Long story short

Long story *Short*

FLASH FICTION BY

SIXTY-FIVE OF NORTH CAROLINA'S

FINEST WRITERS

Edited by Marianne Gingher

The University of North Carolina Press CHAPEL HILL

© 2009
THE UNIVERSITY OF
NORTH CAROLINA PRESS
All rights reserved
Manufactured in the
United States of America
Designed by Kim Bryant
Set in Arnhem by Tseng
Information Systems, Inc.

*The University of North
Carolina Press has been a
member of the Green Press
Initiative since 2003.*

The paper in this book meets the guidelines for
permanence and durability of the Committee on
Production Guidelines for Book Longevity of the
Council on Library Resources.

LIBRARY OF CONGRESS CATALOGING-IN-
PUBLICATION DATA
Long story short : flash fiction by sixty-five
of North Carolina's finest writers / edited by
Marianne Gingher.
p. cm.
ISBN 978-0-8078-3328-5 (cloth : alk. paper) —
ISBN 978-0-8078-5977-3 (pbk. : alk. paper)
1. Short stories, American—North Carolina.
I. Gingher, Marianne.
PS558.N8L645 2009
813'.01089756—dc22   2009002899

cloth   13 12 11 10 09   5 4 3 2 1
paper   13 12 11 10 09   5 4 3 2 1

contents

Acknowledgments

I would never have become a writer or a teacher without the patience, challenges, and inspiration of superb mentors who throughout my life have undertaken to guide me. This book, which I hope will please readers everywhere and find its way into the hands of eager students, writers, and teachers of literature, is dedicated to dauntless North Carolina teachers who continue to make a difference in the lives of the intellectually hungry and curious. Thanks, first and foremost, to Peggy Joyner, my AP English teacher at Grimsley High School, Greensboro; bows and wows ad infinitum to Daphne Athas, Doris Betts, Fred Chappell, and the late Max Steele, lifelong champions of both literature and the literary underdog.

I am grateful for the abiding enthusiasm of my colleagues in the Department of English and Comparative Literature at the University of North Carolina at Chapel Hill, especially Connie Eble, Beverly Taylor, and Linda Wagner-Martin, exemplars of fearlessness, fortitude, and fun; my pals in the Creative Writing Program; and the scholars and artists who joined me around the lively seminar table at the Institute of Arts and Humanities in the spring of 2008 when a fellowship provided by the Max C. Chapman family enabled me to dig into the project that became this anthology.

Thanks to UNC's Research Council and the Office of the Vice Chancellor's Award in Fine Arts and Humanities for grants that supported this endeavor. I am enormously indebted to two smart young women, Tess Tabor and Laura Williamson, both UNC graduates, who helped me in the early stages of hunting and gathering as well as in finalizing the manuscript for publication. Kudos and halos to them both.

Multitudes of gratitude to the folks at the University of North Carolina Press, especially David Perry and Zachary Read for shep-

herding this book into existence and Paula Wald for her meticu-
lous and enthusiastic copyediting. It really does take a village.

Thanks, finally, to the wonderful writers contained in these
pages. That the humble state of North Carolina could have nur-
tured and abetted so many masterful wordsmiths seems an em-
barrassment of riches. Their stories were my inspiration, and I am
delighted to be able to share them.

Introduction

It was the late Max Steele, venerable director of the University of
North Carolina at Chapel Hill's Creative Writing Program from
1967 until his retirement in 1988, who turned me on to the "short-
short" story, variously known as "flash," "sudden," "postcard," or
"micro" fiction; "storybyte"; or "fictoid." In Japan, short-shorts are
known as "palm-of-hand stories." I'd been reading short-shorts all
my life without paying much attention to the fact that because of
their potent brevity, for contemporary readers and writers, they
had gained the niche of a distinct and esteemed subgenre.

So what *is* a "short-short" story besides, well, short? Without
sacrificing intricacy, it lacks digression, subplots, ditherings, and
ornamentations that traditional longer stories accommodate.
Fred Chappell, former poet laureate of North Carolina, has written
that the short-short, besides being less than 2,000 words, should
be "troubling." He goes on to suggest that "*unease*, whether hu-
morous or sad, is the effect that the short-short aims at." Very
short stories frequently give the impression of requiring innova-
tive strategies and unconventional forms, of taking liberties and
risks. One expects them, on the whole, to be playful, like puppies
off leashes, breaking rules. Which rules? I doubt you could cajole
the sixty-five writers assembled between these covers into agreeing
unanimously on any single way to write a short-short. The genre is
a gleefully opportunistic shape-shifter; its appearance on a writer's
blank page can seem serendipitous, a stroke more of luck than of
genius. A hybrid like the gryphon, the short-short is grounded in
prose, but poetic instincts give it wings.

Although the origins of the short-short are obscure, I'd wager
that a snippet of gossip started it all. Storytellers from Aesop to
Hemingway provide powerful examples. If you survey the history
of the short story, you will find that nearly every master of the form

wrote the occasional short-short. Isaac Babel, Anton Chekhov, and Franz Kafka all wrote them, and more recently, American writers like Steve Almond, Donald Barthelme, Richard Brautigan, Raymond Carver, Louise Erdrich, Jamaica Kincaid, W. S. Merwin, Mark Strand, and Elizabeth Tallent have found the short-short a compelling way to merge lyric with narrative, to say something provocative and complete with startling compression and without resorting to irony-loaded trick endings.

The successful short-short is neither prose poem nor vignette; it is not a sketch, riff, or bagatelle. Readers expect it to deliver the gratifications of a longer story, except in a microscopic dose. A short-short is scant but not slight; it is simultaneously rich and fat-free. You tend to go, "Ah-ha!" at the end of one. There's a flash of satisfaction and surprising reward, like finding the tiniest and most exquisite key that unlocks the big glittering kingdom of art.

IN 2002, MAX STEELE returned to the UNC campus as a guest lecturer to share his exuberance for the short-short with our creative-writing students and to establish an annual short-short competition we dubbed the "Mini-Max." Max sponsored the first contest and awarded the top prize of 100 silver dollars, which he presented in a purse that had belonged to his friend and fellow writer Alice Adams. An ardent practitioner of the form himself, he visited classes, reading his own stories and the work of others to illustrate the unique virtues of the form. The students sat spellbound; I sat spellbound. We all wanted to try writing one. It looked easy. But trying to fit a camel-sized theme through a needle's-eye plot was hard. Max offered us impressive lessons about how much we could say in the fewest words. He instructed us in the art of leaving out, which, in our information-saturated age, might turn out to be literature's strongest and most durable new directive.

Inspired by Steele's own late-in-life wonder at this Cracker Jack–prize style of narrative, I determined to honor his legacy as mentor and friend to multiple generations of North Carolina writers by inviting submissions of short-shorts from some of our best and brightest literary lights, from the iconic to the emerging talent, and, in this era of supersizing and hyperbole, challenging writers to advance the cause of the small.

The robust little stories gathered here represent sixty-five contemporary North Carolina writers, admittedly a fraction of the talent thriving throughout our state. The short-shorts are arranged alphabetically by author, for easy reference, with the exception of Max Steele's story, which leads the way. Only writers primarily known for their fiction are included. Every writer in the anthology spent formative years in this state or relocated here. Most still call North Carolina home. Readers will doubtlessly discover that a few significant voices are missing from this book, as are newer writers I've yet to locate. Several authors I solicited declined outright to participate because, as one told me with chagrin, "I don't do short-shorts. I'm a tome person." A few offered "to try" to write something really short ("It will be a challenge!") but got waylaid. One writer trimmed and rewrote his piece diligently but could only squeeze the original draft down to 2,967 words and gave up. I'd mandated a limit of 1,200 words, but as the project gathered steam and amazing submissions in the 1,400–1,500-word range began to arrive, I relaxed my Procrustean standards and caved in to a few sprawlers, and I believe the collection is all the richer for it. Out of the sixty-five entries, more than half are newly minted and have never been published elsewhere. One of the oldest stories, Fred Chappell's "January," was written when he was a graduate student at Duke University. For its small size, it had a monumental influence on Chappell's career. Discussed in a "bootleg writing class" that Reynolds Price put together and that included the young writer Anne Tyler, the story was published in Duke's literary magazine, *The Archive*, and later read by a panel of visiting writers that included Jessie Rehder (who founded the Creative Writing Program at UNC) and an important New York editor, Hiram Haydn. Haydn liked "January," and that "gave me an 'in,'" Chappell reported to me, "when I expanded the one page into my first novel and shipt it to him. And he published it." Imagine a short-short powerful enough to launch a writer's career! Think of Thumbelina as a superhero.

The shortest story in this anthology is Carrie Knowles's "My

Family," a crystalline 95 words. The longest story, "Nero," belongs to Michael Malone and weighs in at a lighthearted 1,678 words. With the exception of a few pieces well under 500 words (stories by Amy Knox Brown, Clyde Edgerton, Margaret Maron, Deborah Seabrooke, Melanie Sumner, and myself), the majority of stories are shorter than 1,200 words. The longest can be read, even savored, in less than ten minutes. Read aloud, they make great bedtime stories for drowsy adults.

From comic surprises in stories by Wendy Brenner, Sarah Dessen, John Kessel, Doug Marlette, Shelia Moses, Lawrence Naumoff, Peggy Payne, Bland Simpson, Lee Smith, Daniel Wallace, and Lynn York to lyrical musings in narratives by Kelly Cherry, Philip Gerard, and Heather Ross Miller, we are reminded *why* we read: to laugh, to learn, to feel, to recognize, to be shaken out of the comfortable and familiar and taken elsewhere, to make connections with the world outside our own skins. Stories like David Rowell's "An Afternoon, No Wind" and Elizabeth Spencer's "The Everlasting Light" are so charming that we nearly forget the vulnerabilities of characters who can't quite articulate their epiphanies. Highlighting the sorrows, joys, revelations, and pratfalls of childhood are Daphne Athas's "Games," Elizabeth Cox's "A Way in a Manger," Quinn Dalton's "Small," Telisha Moore Leigg's "Keening . . . 1 Mile," Jenny Offill's "August," and John Rowell's "The Teachers' Lounge." Doris Betts's "The Girl Who Wanted to Be a Horse" and Angela Davis-Gardner's "The True Daughter" cover decades of estrangement between parents and children in the briefest pages. In contributions by Jill McCorkle and Max Steele, we stand in the long, discomfiting shadow of divorce.

Fans of the fantastical and absurd as well as literature that depicts alternate realities will enjoy imaginative offerings by Orson Scott Card, Jim Grimsley, Philip McFee, and Joe Ashby Porter. Poignant stories by Russell Banks, Pam Durban, and Ruth Moose focus on aging, disenfranchisement, and loss. In her tour de force monologue, "hey brother," Bekah Brunstetter speculates on the personal cost of a sister facing her serviceman brother's imminent departure for Iraq. Yearning and betrayal haunt characters in

Tracie Fellers's "Reverb," Virginia Holman's "Contempt," Randall Kenan's "Where She Sits," and Courtney Jones Mitchell's "How to Roll." Anthony S. Abbott, Ben Fountain, Haven Kimmel, and Peter Makuck write dead-on portraits of adolescent bungling and cruelty, while John McNally and Michael Parker depict boyhood enthrallments with drive-in movies and miniature golf.

Gail Godwin's provocative tale is about the nature of storytelling itself; Wilton Barnhardt, Pamela Duncan, and Denise Rickman write touching portraits of people reckoning with noisy truths about their quiet lives. Will Blythe's extensive obituary, "The End," is both unsettling and grimly funny, somehow taking the measure of human pretense and lame intentions. Settings of stories differ widely, from a zoo in Lydia Millet's "Walking Bird" to a jail cell in Dave Shaw's "The Assistant D.A."; from a hardscrabble mountain community in Robert Morgan's "The Pounding" to a banal, slow-moving grocery line in Elizabeth Oliver's "Line." Cars as symbols of a marriage devolving are at the heart of June Spence's meditative story, glimpses of the ruined American dream are found in the rubble of a car wreck in Luke Whisnant's sobering story, and beautiful music provokes both love and murder in Katherine Min's little gem.

Putting together this anthology of short-shorts, I often felt more like a wedding or reunion planner than an editor. Any reunion is filled with surprises and a shared sense of history and community. And everybody knows that weddings bring out the best and the most outrageous in folks. Some days it felt as if I was having too much fun to be working on a book—these writers are spirited company, both on and off the page!

As I bring this project to a conclusion, I am amazed by the variety and power of these stories, grateful to the authors for their generosity and goodwill, and proud to be living and writing in a state where great storytellers have always thrived, from Sir Walter Raleigh to Thomas Wolfe to contemporary artists of national stature like Russell Banks, Gail Godwin, and Elizabeth Spencer to emerging talents like Denise Rickman, the youngest contributor in this book. From quill pen to word processor, the beat goes on.

I hope that readers not only enjoy the short-shorts gathered here but also feel inspired to look for short-shorts in everyday life, caged in other pages or roaming wild. They seem to be everywhere, whether by design or happenstance: flashes of grace, moments of reckoning, fierce and marvelous.

Long story short

The Playhouse

Max Steele

The professor was standing now before the doors of the American Embassy. He was early for an appointment with an old frat brother, a legal attaché who would help him procure a fast Mexican divorce. There was no urgency really in getting a divorce. It was simply that he could not concentrate on a permanent separation. When he tried he would end up in a hot soapy shower thinking about putting on freshly starched cotton clothes. Someone should have warned him in Raleigh not to drink on the plane. Here he was in Mexico City, a mile high, still a bit dazed.

Three blond children, not more than five or six years old, obviously embassy kids, a little girl and two little boys, were playing house in and around a sort of blueprint design of squares and rectangles drawn with green chalk on the sidewalk. A solid block of taxicabs, more than the professor had ever seen, was passing on the Paseo de la Reforma.

Something about the broad boulevards and the taxi horns reminded him strongly of Paris, where twenty years ago he had spent his one sabbatical. The next year he had met his wife, who often reminded him that he had never taken her to Paris as he had promised. Or done any fun things. There was never enough money on his salary, she accused him, to do any fun things. In the late autumn air the feeling of déjà vu was so strong that he felt it was a dream, or a forgotten passage from a novel he was living through.

The two boys were now standing near him whispering, and the little girl was in the chalk-line house, busily sweeping, putting things on shelves, getting pots out of a stove only she could see, and washing dishes in the silent sink.

At a signal he did not notice, the small boys, giggling and full of

1

themselves, marched slowly to the front of the house and knocked on the door. "Knock. Knock."

The little girl seemed genuinely surprised. She came through the house, untying her apron and opened the door, drying her hands on the apron.

"Oh, there you are!" She was quite annoyed. "Late again, as usual. And furthermore you have brought a perfect stranger home to dinner." Oh, she was vexed. "Without even asking. Without even calling!"

"Yes, my dear," the little husband said proudly, full of his secret. "I would like for you to meet the man who owns the merry-go-round."

As the boys entered the house, the professor glanced at his watch. He was still five minutes early. Enough time to walk to the far corner.

As he strolled up the dark gusty boulevard, he could still hear the high laughter of the children, and at the sound of their thin, excited voices his heart almost broke. After all, how were they to know (for they were still children), how could he have known she would run off with the man who owned the merry-go-round?

The Roommate

Anthony S. Abbott

David's roommate in the third-form dorm at the Wicker School for Boys was Jackie Callaghan. During the first weeks of school the two saw little of each other. David got up at the rising bell in the morning, showered, and left for breakfast before Jackie was even awake. Jackie always waited for the warning bell, the five-minute bell. He threw on his clothes, tying his tie and tucking in his shirt as he flew toward the dining hall, guarded by two sixth-form monitors. If you were late you had to run the triangle—the triangular route from the dining hall to the soccer field, then down the highway and back across the base of the mountain to the dining hall again. It took fifteen minutes. When you got back, you could eat unless the food was gone. Then you went hungry, unless a friend saved you something.

Jackie made David nervous. At night Jackie rushed into the room two minutes before lights-out and changed into his pajamas in the dark. When the bell rang, the sixth formers shined their flashlights in to be sure there was a body in each bed.

At first Jackie teased David. "Come on," he would say after the sixth-form bed check, "tell me something you've done that was bad. Come on, Mister goody-goody, let's hear about your exploits. Like how you got a B once or something really terrible."

But when David didn't respond, Jackie got tired of the game. Then, one particular day in October, just after lights out, there was a furious pounding on all the doors.

"All right, you little stinkers, everyone out in the hall, on the double," came the voice of Harry Young, otherwise known as "Mighty Joe Young." He was a wrestler, he had hair on his chest and back, and he was the third-form dorm prefect.

They stood in a line, each of them, backs to the wall, next to their own doors.

"Everybody down," said Mighty Joe Young.

Everybody squatted.

"Now duckwalk, down to the end of the hall and back to your rooms twice."

No one started.

"Move!" said the prefect. "Move!" echoed his assistants, a couple of lesser sixth formers.

The boys moved, down and back, then down and back again until their legs ached, then they stood again next to their doors.

"Now listen!" said the prefect. "This hall stinks. This hall smells. And this is what we do to stinkers, to smelly bastards who don't take showers."

He started at the end of the hall, walked by David and Jackie, then stopped. He touched Barry LeMaster on the shoulder. "You," he said. "Strip!"

They turned their heads, ever so slightly, to see what was happening. Barry didn't move. Mighty Joe's hands reached toward the boy. Each hand grasped a lapel of Barry's pajamas and yanked hard. The boy's pajama top burst apart, buttons clattering on the hard floor. Mighty Joe wrenched it off the boy's shoulders and down his arms, leaving him shivering.

"Now the bottom," he said.

It was cruel and therefore wrong, David knew, but there was something strangely exciting about it too, something dark and dangerous. He watched as the boy dropped his pants and then ran for the shower room, holding his hands in front of his exposed genitals. The sixth formers followed him inside. When he came out, his skin was pink and his eyes had the glazed look of a steer being led to slaughter.

"Now, get in your rooms, all of you, and let this be a lesson," said Mighty Joe.

They turned and started into their rooms.

"Not you, Callaghan," said Mighty Joe. "You wait."

David climbed into bed and pulled the covers up. He was afraid of what they might do to Jackie. It began to make sense, Jackie's sleeping late in the morning, his undressing in the dark. Maybe he didn't want anybody to see him. The showers were public, three or four at a time. He had never seen Jackie in the showers either in the morning or after sports.

When Jackie came in, David turned to look at him across the room.

"What happened, Jackie?" he asked.

"Last warning," Jackie said softly. "Next time it's me."

"Then do it, Jackie. What's wrong with taking showers?"

"I won't let those bastards tell me what to do. That's why," he hissed. "It's fine for you. You like it here, I can tell. Mister fucking rise-and-shine."

David didn't know what to say.

"You like it here, don't you?" Jackie continued. "I didn't want to be here in the first place. They can do what they want, but I'm damned if I'll kowtow to that hairy brute."

"It's just a shower," David said quietly.

"Just a shower! Just a shower! For Christ's sake, don't you stand for anything? You just do everything they say, and pretty soon, there's nothing left of you. You've got to draw a line somewhere, OK? This is mine."

It didn't make sense to David, to draw a line over a shower. Still, Jackie's words echoed in his heart—"pretty soon, there's nothing left of you."

Two nights later they came for him. "Bring your towels," Harry Young shouted as he pounded on the door.

David hesitated, then grabbed his towel and walked into the hall.

"You're a real bastard," Jackie Callaghan said to David as he passed.

David waited in the hall terrified. If Jackie didn't come out on his own, they would go in and drag him out. David didn't want to see that. He didn't want any part of the whole thing, but there was nothing to be done, nothing to be achieved by fighting. And then Jackie's words again, "pretty soon, there's nothing left of you,"

5

and Jackie being dragged down the hall, naked except for his white underpants, a sixth former shouldering each arm. They turned into the shower room, and David could see the limp legs disappearing behind the door.

After ten minutes Jackie came out, dripping wet, a towel around his middle, and he walked slowly down the hall toward David as all the third formers started flicking their towels at him. That was the routine. If you had been warned and you did not comply, you got the towel treatment.

David couldn't stand it. He broke ranks, ran toward Jackie. The next thing he knew there was a hairy arm around his neck choking him.

"Look, buddy," growled Mighty Joe Young. "Don't you ever disobey me." And the prefect grabbed David with both hands, shoved him against the wall, then yanked him back and shoved again, yanked and shoved until David slumped to the floor. "And if you say anything about this, any of you, you're all dead meat. Now get to bed."

For a while Jackie and David just sat there on the floor outside their room, side by side, their backs against the wall. Then Jackie laughed. "Not bad for a goody-goody, not bad for a fucking sheep. I gotta hand it to you." They helped each other up and went to bed.

The next day Jackie Callaghan was gone.

Games

Daphne Athas

One summer our father painted a white cross on a turtle's shell. He said the turtle carried its house wherever it went and would live over a hundred years, which meant we'd be dead first. We didn't believe that though. We were too young, our oldest brother only eleven. He told us that we owned the turtle because if we let it wander free on its fat leather feet through the rhubarb garden next to the pond, every year when we looked for it we would find it and recognize its white cross and greet its everlasting turtle life.

Later, on another summer afternoon when we were in our rooms upstairs, he called to us from the hallway, "Quick! Come outdoors!" He had Mother's opera glasses in his hand. We clopped loudly down the stairs after him.

Above our backyard we saw the German zeppelin *Hindenburg* following the coastline south. It was a dot shining in the sky, a peculiarity in daytime. He said that its fat shell was made of canvas filled with helium gas making it float, and that people were sitting in luxurious seats inside the tube, small as Kolynos toothpaste, hitched to its bottom. He let us look, but it was hard to see through opera glasses. It hung there motionless and didn't move forward, so we got bored. Why was Daddy excited?

Three weeks later it exploded in a fiery, flapping skin of gas above New Jersey. Some of the people were burned to crisps. How shocked we were! We pored over the brown photographs in the rotogravure section. The oval balloon-shape was only a bit longer than the turtle's shell, but instead of feet, flames like tongues were leaping out of it in huge orange breaths.

"What stops first when you die—lungs, heart, liver, or what?" Daddy asked us at breakfast. His teaching was incidental, and he

7

waited for us to answer, but we always knew because he told us beforehand. "Everything stops at the same time," we repeated in unison, "because everything is connected to everything else."

"Yes, only stupid people conceive of life in pieces," came his response to this litany. Though modern medicine might dispute that now, at the time it was our paradigm. Breath was the key.

We breathed hard when he taught us directions, making us face north toward Portland. "Hold out your arms," he said, showing us that our right hand pointed east, our left hand west, and our back south. We breathed with waves and tide, copying him as he demonstrated with his arms outstretched too. His jaw was a promontory against the Atlantic. He was practically bald, his face as brown as Braces Rock, his nose sharp, his skin swarthy, and his mouth wide and sculpted. His eyes, encased below sun-bleached eyebrows, were deep set and ice-blue. You had to look hard to find the him in them, and sometimes they were remote, sometimes porous, for he was a reflector rather than a gatherer.

"Superstitious boobs think that when you breathe your last breath the soul comes out of your nose and mouth and rises to heaven. Breath," he announced, "is not soul." He was a naturalized citizen, and this was his immigrant's protest against the chants and smells of olive oil and myrrh of his bringing-up in the Greek Orthodox Church. But his propaganda for American science backfired, for by saying it out loud, soul became identified with breath.

We were playing in the living room one Sunday and he was reading. We crawled over to his chair, rose, leaned against his knees, and peeped at him over his newspaper. He ignored us, so we batted the newspaper out of his hands. He dropped from his chair, thudding onto the floor next to it.

We laughed, but he didn't move. We poked him gently, but he remained inert. He refused to move. He refused to look at us. We got down and swarmed on him like Lilliputians, knocking on his polished shoes, pulling his nose, and laughing. We changed his arm from one position to another where it lay limp as clay. We pulled one foot up and put it down, and then we changed the posi-

8

tion of his right leg. His black sock profiled a magnificent ankle coasting its lonely way down into the leather shoe. He polished this shoe every day with oxblood, which contrasted blood-brown against sporty, black pinpoint decorative holes. The silence was terrible.

We got scared. We punched him experimentally. He didn't resist, so we hollered into his face, "Come out!" but he didn't. "Come out!" we pleaded again and waited a long time. Not knowing what else to do, we gingerly pulled one eyelid up to force him to see us. His blue eyeball rolled upward to heaven, leaving the white.

We could put our hand over his mouth to suffocate him, we knew, but we didn't dare, so we started hitting him again, harder. He would have to move for he was powerless; we could make him die.

We were afraid. Then we got mad.

Guiltily we backed away, but he sensed our moment of abandonment and opened one eye, which looked at us quite clearly but without recognition. Then he got up and without a glance walked away, as if he had never been dead.

The Outer Banks

Russell Banks

The man pulled the RV off the road and parked it in a small paved lot, the front bumper kissing the concrete barrier, the large, pale-gray vehicle facing the sea, and his wife said, "Why are we stopping?" The rain came in curtains off the Atlantic, one after the other, like the waves breaking against the sand, only slower, neither building nor diminishing, passing over them rhythmically. They watched through the wide, flat windshield. There were no other vehicles in the lot and none in sight on the coastline road behind them. It was late fall, and the summer houses and rental cottages and motels were closed for the season.

"I don't know why. I mean, I do know. Because of the dog." He relighted the cold stub of his cigar, and for a long while the couple sat in silence, watching the rain come in.

Finally she said, "So these are the famous Outer Banks of North Carolina."

"Yeah, I'm sorry about the weather," he said. "Graveyard of the Atlantic."

"Yes. I know."

"Joke, Alice? Joke?"

She didn't answer him. A moment passed and he said, "We've got to do something about the dog. You know that?"

"What've you got in mind? Bury her in the sand? That's a real cute idea, Ed. Bury her in the sand and drive on our merry way, just like that." She looked at her hands for a moment. "I don't like thinking about it either, you know."

He eased himself from his chair, stood uncertainly, and walked back through the living area and the tidy galley to the closet-sized bathroom, where he got down carefully on his knees and drew back the shower curtain and looked at the body of their dog. It was a black-and-white mixed-breed—lab and springer, they'd been told—grizzled, lying on her side where Ed had found her this morning, when, naked, he'd gone to take a shower. He studied the dog's stiffened muzzle. "Poor bastard," he said.

"Maybe we should try to find a vet!" she called to him from the front.

"She's dead, Alice!" he hollered back.

"They'll know how to take care of her, I meant."

Ed stood up. He was seventy-two; the simplest things had gotten very difficult very quickly—standing up, sitting down, getting out of bed, driving for longer than four or five hours. When they left home barely a year ago, none of those things had been difficult for him. That was why he'd done it, left home, why they both had done it, because nothing simple was especially difficult for them, yet they were old enough to know that whatever they did not do or see now they would never do or see at all, ever.

It was her idea, too, not his alone—the romance of the open road, see America and die, master of your destiny, all that—although the actual plan had been his, to sell the house in Troy and all their furniture, to buy and outfit the RV, map and follow the interstate from upstate New York to Disney World to the Grand Canyon to Yosemite to the Black Hills—man, he'd always wanted to go see the Black Hills of Dakota, and Mount Rushmore was even grander and more inspirational than he'd hoped—then on to Graceland, and now the Outer Banks. He hadn't once missed the hardware store, and she hadn't missed the bank. They'd looked forward to retirement and, once there, had liked it, as if it were a vacation spot and they'd decided to stay year-round. There were no children or grandchildren or other close family—they were free as birds. "Snowbirds," they'd been called in Florida and out in Arizona. When they left home, their dog, Rosie, had been old, ten or eleven, he wasn't sure, they'd gotten her from the pound, but, Jesus, he hadn't figured on her dying like this. It was as if she'd run out of air, out of life, like a watch that had run down because someone forgot to wind it.

He dropped his cigar butt into the toilet, looked at it for a second, and resisted flushing—she'd scowl when she saw it, he knew, because it was ugly, even he thought so, but he shouldn't waste the water. Then he walked heavily back to the front and sat in the driver's seat.

"Vets are for sick animals. Not dead animals," he said to her.

"I suppose you want to leave her in a Dumpster or just drop her at the side of the road somewhere."

"We should have found a home for Rosie. When we left Troy. Should've given her to some people or something, you know?" He looked at his wife as if for a solution. She was crying, though. Silently, with tears streaming down her pale cheeks, she cried steadily, as if she had been crying for a long time and had no idea how to stop.

He put a hand on her shoulder. "Alice. Hey, c'mon, don't cry. Jesus, it's not the end of the world."

She stopped and fumbled in the glove compartment for a tissue, found one, and wiped her face. "I know. But what are we going to do?"

"About what?"

"Oh, Ed. About Rosie, *This*," she said, and waved a hand at the rain and the sea. "Everything."

"It's my fault," he said. He stared at her profile, hoping she would turn to him and say no, it wasn't his fault, it wasn't anybody's. But she didn't turn to him; she said nothing.

Slowly, he rose from his seat again. He walked to the bathroom and pulled back the shower curtain. He kneeled down and gently lifted the dog in his arms, surprised that she was not heavier. Lying there, she had seemed solid and heavy, as if carved of wood and painted, like an old merry-go-round horse. He carried the dog to the side door of the RV and worked it open with his knee and stepped down to the pavement. The rain fell on him and he was quickly drenched. He wore only a short-sleeved shirt and Bermuda shorts and sneakers, and he was cold all of a sudden. He carried the dog to the far corner of the parking lot, stepped over the barrier to the beach, and walked with slow, careful steps through the wet sand toward the water. The rain blocked his vision and plastered white swatches of his hair to his skull and his thin clothes to his body.

Halfway between the parking lot and the water, he stopped and set the dog down. He was breathing rapidly from the effort. He wiped the rain from his eyes, got down on his hands and knees, and started scooping sand. He pulled double handfuls of it away, working down through the wet, gray sand to the dry sand beneath, and kept digging until finally he had carved a large hole. Still on his knees, he reached across the hole and drew the body of the dog into it. Her hair was wet and smelled the way it had when she was still alive. Then slowly, carefully, he covered her.

When he was finished and there was a low mound where before there had been a hole, he turned around and looked back at the RV in the parking lot. He could see his wife staring out the windshield from the passenger's seat. He couldn't tell if she was looking at him or at the sea or what. He turned his gaze toward the sea. The rain was still coming heavily in curtains, one after the other.

He stood and brushed the crumbs of wet sand from his clothes, bare legs, and hands and made his way back to the parking lot. When he had settled himself into the driver's seat, he said to his wife, "That's the end of it. I don't want to hear anymore about it. OK?" He turned the ignition key and started the motor. The windshield wipers swept back and forth like wands.

"OK," she said.

He backed the RV around and headed toward the road. "You hungry?" he asked her.

She spoke slowly, as if to herself. "There's supposed to be a good seafood place a few miles south of here. It's toward Kitty Hawk. So that's good."

He put the RV into gear and pulled out of the lot onto the road south. "Fine," he said. "Too bad we have to see Kitty Hawk in the rain, though. I was looking forward to seeing it. I mean, the Wright brothers and all."

"I know you were," she said. The cumbersome vehicle splashed along the straight two-lane highway, and no cars passed. Everyone else seemed to be inside today, staying home.

stoma

Wilton Barnhardt

My career at Mecklenburg County General has been a parade of
vagrants, crack addicts (poor and black), meth addicts (poor and
white), and lots of vomiters—they always give me the vomiters. The
food-poisoned, the toddler who got into the ammonia under the
sink, the UNC-C freshman a minute from an alcoholic coma.

"Hey O'Connell!" the ER desk chief cries from his station.
"Looks like Henry needs a bath!" He thinks these kind of stick-it-
to-the-new-boy assignments are a yuckfest, each and every time.

The attendings and older residents pat my shoulder, assure me
that back when they were new they suffered lots lots worse . . . and
then I'll prod Homeless Henry along to the shower room to strip
off his clothes, caked with a month of body waste, hose him down,
soap him up, start treating his wounds, which, thanks to the dia-
betes, won't be healing anytime soon or probably ever.

"Hey O'Connell!" Here we go again. "Guess who we got today?
Your *boyfriend's* here!" One of the Admitting comedians lets his
wrist go limp and throws his head back girlishly to the amusement
of everyone.

It's Angel, who is a legend. The name mentioned most when the
residents in the breakroom review their catalog of worsts and most-
disgustings. Male prostitute. Latin or maybe mixed race, maybe
thirty years old. HIV-positive and not taking the cocktail, or not
taking it regularly, according to Social Services. Sometimes it was
Karposi lesions, sometimes scabs that wouldn't heal, staph and
lice from living on the street, malnutrition, every STD in the book
and a few that hadn't been heard of until he dragged them in.

"Exam room three," says Rosa, the nurse practitioner who will
accompany me. She is training Pilar, and they both do much of this

training in Spanish, so I have no idea what's really being said about me or my patients half the time.

"Evening, ladies," says Angel, including me in that.

Angel is missing teeth from crack addiction, and rather ugly to begin with despite attempts at prettification with a wig or makeup, an *ensemble* gotten at Goodwill or from a trashcan, short skirts, ruffled tops, a reeking tattered red raincoat that looks to have been made out of sofa material (perfect for absorbing every stain of the street and sex trade), and, so I understand, a new acquisition, a white feather boa that looks as if it had been dragged down the gutters of Park Road, where the Charlotte hustlers too poor for internet access now lurk in the shadows of a city park.

Angel saunters to an exam table, shedding clothes, wasting no time.

There had been, some years back, a vicious misadventure with a client who, failing to get an erection for Angel, used a broken beer bottle to consummate their union. The damage to Angel's colon was too great, so it was removed and he wore a colostomy bag. Social Services provides new sanitary supplies, not that Angel stops by Social Services too much. I inspect my latex gloves to make sure there's no tear, and I sit on a rolling stool and examine the stoma where the bag is attached.

"Ow," Angel says when I peel away the flange and the filthy wafer bandage. There was inflammation, redness, and oozy blisters . . . "Sweetheart," Angel says steadily, "just give me some of that antibiotic stuff y'all always give me."

"This isn't from gonorrhea," I mumble, revolted by the smell. "These are number two herpes simplex and that's a virus. How could this area come in contact with genital . . ."

I stop as the implication of my half-question occurs to me.

Angel says nothing.

"*Madre de Dios*," says Rosa under her breath. Pilar shakes her head.

Angel stares straight ahead, lips pursed. Finally, he rolls his eyes, barely moving a facial muscle. "Well. The guy said he wanted to . . ." Then Angel sighs with just a touch of weariness, looking

15

warmly at me. "C'mon baby doctor, can you give your Angel some cream or some'n?"

Naturally, the nurses spread Angel's newest malady around the ER, and I think the whole hospital was aware of it before the shift was out. There was giddy mock-horror, lots of that dark laughter with which people in the medical profession buffer and shield themselves, with a patented dose of judgment. We like it, in hospitals, when people die from what they did. Smoking, drinking, getting fat, unsafe sex—they asked for it, A led to B, case closed, so much easier than when it's an unearned death or a disease-worse-than-death dropped out of the sky, SIDS, a child dead by a stray gunshot, a teenager with an aneurysm, pancreatic cancer, ALS, Huntington's chorea—those deaths don't get the laugh track. No, Angel is a godsend. He's gonna get what's coming to him and they can all feel good about that.

But when my shift is over and I'm trying to sleep, and like so many nights I'm too tired to just lose consciousness, I think about how Angel did not blink or draw an uneven breath as he stared straight ahead, not a fleeting second of shame or regret. Maybe that's the face he has to put out to the world, maybe he's lost the capacity for regret, or maybe if he starts regretting there will come a flood of other things until his whole life piles up in the balance on the other side, but I'd like to think it's his real face, burnished and polished by life and rough handling and maybe, because I'm gay too, I want to think when the guy was paying to do what he did, Angel found some small keepsake coin of pleasure in it if only in the consent, not all that different from the first consent, the first time, just kissing another boy, both of you drunk in the backseat of a car after a high school football game, when that was as dangerous as anything ever attempted but you tried it because you hoped it might bring you the consuming fulfillment that a wounded life had so far denied, puncturing all the falsity of the rest, and maybe it was like that, maybe it was good for just a second because it recalled that young-forever hope that says *I dunno, I guess we could try it*, heroic in its way before it goes wrong and goes bad, has consequences and humiliations, the way love does us all.

. . . .

The Girl Who Wanted to Be a Horse

Doris Betts

Something was wrong with Amanda and Mother had a word for it—grief.

Now age six, Amanda had lost her father last year to a heart attack. Some thought his heart might have dried to a husk, from starvation; Amanda's Mother was not popular in the neighborhood. She corrected everyone's grammar. She made vocabulary suggestions.

Besides "grief" assigned to Amanda, Mother had a word for herself as well: guilt. After a year, she had been unable to find and wed a father-substitute. An English teacher, she perhaps overvalued words and talked as much to Amanda now as she had to her dead husband. Amanda rarely answered. The girl grew shy, then quiet, then lethargic and almost mute—the worst thing Mother could imagine.

First grade did not help, nor did playgrounds or parks or zoos. Chattering playmates were imported, but Amanda remained silent.

At last horseback lessons stirred her first enthusiasm. Mother was relieved to hear, at least, "Hey!" "Whoa!" and "Attaboy!"

When beginner riders were at last allowed to practice low jumps, Amanda not only leaned over the gelding's neck as taught, but clasped both arms there and pressed her face into the mane. It was as if she were trying to melt herself into the horse. She neglected to rein him in after landing, and the teacher could barely unfuse the two surfaces and haul her body off the saddle. More lessons occurred, but Amanda's clinging habit grew worse and they were finally stopped.

Mother enrolled her next in the swim team, tried modern dance, invited girls for sleepovers, even spent more money than her salary warranted on a trip to Disneyland. Amanda's obsession with horses never waned. No matter how much Mother lectured and made lists and offered books on other subjects, Amanda pinned pictures of Derby winners to her bedroom walls. Horses of every breed filled her scrapbooks. Appreciating them was all well and good, Mother said, but it was as if she wanted to *become* a horse. Horses didn't even bark.

Smaller pets were tried—the puppies and kittens and gerbils, to change the subject, even a talking parrot (though it was a shock to learn how long parrots lived; an owner would die while the colorful bird kept asking grandchildren for crackers).

Mother next tried reading up on horses herself, learning the lingo. She could tell the difference between a purebred and a thoroughbred, name the bridles and saddle parts, and even identify horse parasites, which were disgusting.

Another disgusting piece of information was phlegming: the way a horse will react to some pungent odor, throwing the head high and folding the thick upper lip pink above the gum. Even a whiff of perfume could produce the grimace, which most observers translated as "PEW-EE."

One day Mother found Amanda in front of her mirror holding with pinched finger and thumb her own upper lip as high as it would go. The effort seemed pitiful since she had recently lost her baby incisors; she had not been grateful when the tooth fairy left a dictionary under her pillow.

If I'd only remarried, thought Mother, I wouldn't have a neurotic child. If she would talk to me, even write messages. If she had a bigger vocabulary, we could get to the root of our problems.

Direct action came next. Mother took down Amanda's horse photographs and gave to the local library *Black Beauty*, *My Friend Flicka*, *The Red Pony*, et al. She pruned from the video shelf such films as *National Velvet* and *Seabiscuit*. She hid the thick scrapbooks with their racetrack photos, their head shots of Smarty Pants and Barbaro. She removed the oversized painting of Pegasus. She steadily refused to drive Amanda to stables, horse shows, any parade with a horse in it, any cowboy movie.

"Let's talk about other things," she insisted, and did.

Nothing worked. Mother saw a revival of Peter Shaffer's play *Equus*, in which a boy named Alan Strang had his own obsession with horses. The theme was rather dark, and all she took away from it was the hope that since the boy in the play had seen a psychiatrist, Amanda might also benefit.

(It was just like Mother to assume that life could be cured by literature.)

The psychiatrist may have had many helpful words to exchange with Amanda but had little to tell Mother, despite her many questions. He finally mentioned the sexual implications between girls and horses, especially around puberty; grief may have rushed Amanda.

Usually Mother could not decide which adjective best suited her parenting. Did he mean she was controlling? Indulgent? Too demanding? Neglectful? If she could find the right word, she would understand.

By then Amanda had taken to sleeping nights on one side, with arms and legs stiffly extended in lieu of four legs with hooves; and she sometimes tasted grass blades or gave a low whuffle noise. Her dark hair grew long. She ran a lot through the neighborhood, trying to make her hair stream out behind.

Time inched ahead. That doctor and others who followed said Amanda had improved but she was a natural introvert. She would never be much of a talker. By the time she entered her teens, therapy had at least taught her seldom to mention horses at home. Or anything else. She became as still herself as a Trojan Horse, with who knew what inside. Even in school she was still and quiet, and she did not excel.

Mother talked for them both. She explained Amanda to her teachers, to strangers, aloud to herself. She could put in a nutshell what the specialists overcomplicated—how Amanda had suffered a psychic blow from her father's death, and it had silenced her.

At fifteen, Amanda ran away from home.

Just as no one had been able to make her talk, could force no real renouncing of horses, no one could find her, either. For weeks Mother could often be seen on television pleading for her daughter's safe return. She gave interviews, made posters that were long on text and short on pictures. When school let out for the first summer, Mother took long trips on which she might meet Amanda by happenstance. Perhaps by now her daughter had become a circus rider, a groom, an equine veterinarian. Though Mother considered marriage several times, none of her prospects could solve the *Sunday Times* crossword without help, and they drifted away.

Years passed. Mother grew deaf—the best of available old-age options. During all her years she had listened to very few people, and rarely to good effect.

One summer she was on a historical walking tour of Boston, still showing as she always did a very old photograph of Amanda in breeches and riding hat. It was getting dark when she wandered away from her fellow tourists into a ratty neighborhood where many women, the age Amanda might now be, were strolling the sidewalks. The wind was too cool for the very short skirts they wore.

Talking loudly to summarize her daughter's life, Mother stopped a police car and thrust the old photograph inside. With one hand she gestured across the street toward the women moving slowly past.

The officer shook his head, but he also pointed to them. "Whores," he said. "They're whores." He could tell by Mother's too loud voice that she must be hard of hearing, so he said the word louder, "WHORES."

And of course Mother misunderstood. From his car she lurched in an uneven run across the street, mouthing a long string of familiar, empty promises, and calling these toward the women who knew too well their own ways of riding and being ridden.

....

The End

Will Blythe

He died slowly enough in Salisbury to realize that the woman he loved dearly in spite of having slept with her three best bridge part-ners had shot him dead in the surprise of his life. She died in a car crash in Siler City in the midst of a late, happy marriage to a vol-unteer coach for the high school football team. He died without a scrap of poetry in him. They died of carbon-monoxide poisoning from a faulty heater that he claimed to have fixed but, for some reason he himself did not understand, never did. He died unsure of whether he was in heaven or on drugs. She died in her hospital bed in Charlotte, admiring her own hair, which had been one of the glories of her life and which her daughter was brushing hard enough to hurt her scalp. He died having lost his faith in God on September 6, 1970, and never having regained it, a fact that he kept from everyone, raising his children to be honest above all, good Presbyterians in love with God and most people.

He died at eighty-seven, still torn up that he had traded away that blue stamp from Samarkand in the winter of 1944. She died in her condominium, expiring in her sleep, dreaming that she lay next to the man she really loved, her first cousin Jim, a doctor from Cornelius who had married a real witch. He died propped up in the backyard by his beloved wife so that he could watch the Tears of Perseus streak through the August skies, just as the couple had done when first courting, though then his wife had rested her head on his shoulder. She died hearing a symphony that had not yet been written. They died when he took that curve on the highway outside of Winston-Salem too fast, a curve that in years of driving had never failed to please him as he leaned the car hard into it and felt the thrill of physics surging through his thoroughly mortal body.

She died of what was said to be old age, and nobody felt the need to be any more specific than that because she had no next of kin and within three years nobody ever thought about her again for the rest of time. He died conscious that he might have been the last boy in Perquimans County to have shaken the hand of a man who'd been a slave. He died hating just about every white person he'd ever met, except for Franklin Delano Roosevelt, whom he had helped set down in his wheelchair from the train to the platform. He died of a massive coronary while trying to sneak his ball from the rough on the ninth hole of Pinehurst #2, leaving the other members of his foursome in a quandary about whether to joke about this with his widow. She died of cancer, high on morphine, talking to her husband, who was dead himself and in whom she'd been disappointed for the last forty or so years of their marriage after a glorious beginning that maybe set the bar too high.

They died in a house fire in West Durham after everybody passed out and the baby, looking for someone warm to lay against, knocked over a kerosene space heater. He died, the last old-time fiddler in Anson County, poisoned by a member of the Baptist choir, whose secret recipe for pound cake included arsenic. He died the family patriarch, worried that his sons and daughters had lost their way with all their talk about lower taxes and illegal immigrants, though he still loved them very much. She died eaten up by stomach cancer and envy, the envy secretly enjoyed by her best friend, who took it as a tribute to her own happy marriage and expensive house on Lake Norman. She died in the lunchroom of Odell Elementary School the day after everyone forgot her birthday, choking to death on three chicken nuggets, a food the PTA then voted off the menu for an indefinite period.

She died at Carol Woods in Chapel Hill, having never understood why sex was such a big deal and having resisted psychoanalysis since her mid-twenties. He died at home in October of emphysema, hooked up to an oxygen tank, on a night with the harvest moon high above the carport, reminding him briefly of his years deer-hunting back when he could still walk—*oh, walking*! He died of a word his wife could never pronounce. He died of exposure when he followed the family monkey into the tobacco fields one January night; the next day the monkey came home, no worse for the wear, and was imprisoned in the basement until a childless couple from New York took him in.

She died in the nursing home after running out of things to read. They died in the crash of a light plane in the Pisgah National Forest with the pilot in the middle of telling a story about a guy who'd been in his fraternity who had slept with the pilot's wife and the pilot could never tell the story without pretending that this had happened before their marriage rather than in the middle of it and he was in the middle of telling this story that he had not been able to get out of his head for years when the plane hit the trees and then the mountain so hard that he never had the chance to think about how this might have been a parable of sorts about not paying attention. He died terrified of infinity.

She died of Alzheimer's with her three sons arrayed around the hospital bed; she couldn't remember their names, but there was the tall one, the funny one, and the one she loved with silent, unfathomable passion for which words had never been sufficient. They died having kept the secret. He died when the trench collapsed on him many years before he had made enough money to build a house for his wife and children in the state of Puebla. She died transfixed by dust motes turning this way and that in the sunlight of late afternoon. He died of blunt impact trauma, which caused his wife to scandalize their children and the minister when she said, "That amazes me because he was the hardest-headed man I ever knew." She died with words floating into her mind from nowhere.

He died sure that he was going to be famous one day and that his dying before this fame arrived would be a poignant part of a story that would be told forever. She died having worried her whole life about being Jewish though nobody suspected because she worked hard at seeming transparent and some of her closest friends actually believed she was anti-Semitic. He died with the car keys in his pocket digging into his thigh where he lay on the floor, and this sensation was the last thing he ever experienced. She died at her own hand, a vast relief from the tedium that she'd tried to kill with the drinking that had then become its own tedium. He died in Hurdle Mills, sprawled out in the little front yard, having waited twenty-three years for an apology that never came. She died believing that if she just kept living, she would find a way not to die; it was simply impossible to believe otherwise.

They died in a bus accident off I-95 south of the Virginia border, rolling down the embankment into the woods and seeing Jesus somewhat earlier than they had planned, according to the Free Will Baptist minister, who was also the driver of the bus and whose absolute faith in the midst of so much death made him seem like a monster to the husband of one of the deceased. She died enjoying one last cigarette that she knew wasn't going to kill her because the phenobarbital was. He died on the shuttle bus at Raleigh-Durham airport after hearing a beautiful woman with a midwestern accent who was talking on her cell phone say, "Dude, we fucked on the floor," which in an instant made her seem not just ordinary but awful. He died alone, struck by a happiness that seemed to have nothing to do with the circumstances of his life.

Nipple

Wendy Brenner

In the cafeteria fourth period Lori said she had her Uncle Bert's nipple in an envelope. We were all like, What are you talking about, and she was like, I'm not kidding, his nipple fell off and I got it and he doesn't even know I have it. We were all like, screaming, except Meghan, who was like, Right, I'm sure your own nipple falls off and you don't even notice. Lori was like, It's in my locker, I'd be delighted to show you if you don't believe me, and Meghan was like, Woo, *delighted*, well excuse me, Miss Manners, why don't you send out embroidered invitations and hold a ceremony? Then she stood up and left because she had to make up dissecting a fetal pig from when she had mono. Lori was like, What's her problem.

The rest of us were like, Just ignore her, so how did you get his nipple, and Lori goes, I found it in the shower, stuck in the drain thing, I almost stepped on it. Andrea was like, In five seconds I'm going to throw up. I was like, How do you know that's what it is, how do you know it's not a scab, or something, like, else? And Lori was like, Well, he visits every year from Canada and he always walks around without his shirt on, 'cause in the morning he does, like, the Canadian Air Force exercises or something, so every year I've been like *noticing* that his one nipple looks like it's hanging on a thread. It wasn't like bleeding or anything, it was just like, not *attached* all the way. The other one was fine, but that one was like, falling off. I've been waiting for it to fall off for like, three years.

Why was it like that, I asked her. Was he born with it that way or did something happen? Did he get it caught in something, like a zipper or a stapler or something?

Andrea stood up and was like, Excuse me, I am literally going to throw up now. We watched her leave, but she was heading toward

25

the vending machines, not the bathrooms. She's like in love with Junior Mints. Lori was like, I have no idea how it got that way, but I knew it was going to fall off eventually.

All of a sudden, Michelle was like, Wait, oh my God, remember, weren't you telling us that time about how your uncle got hit by lightning on a totally clear day playing horseshoes at a wedding and how now he's thirsty all the time and he never gets cold and he knows stuff before it happens? Well, maybe it happened when the lightning hit him, maybe it hit him exactly on his nipple, or even if it hit him on his back, wouldn't that be strong enough to make his nipple fall off?

But Lori said no, that was her other uncle. Michelle was like, Oh. Then she stood up and said she had to go because she had a conference with Mr. Stirnad, the new guidance counselor who's like never brushed his teeth in his life, and we were like, Bye, don't forget your gas mask.

So then it was just me and Lori sitting there, waiting for the bell to ring, and I was like, So are you going to mail it to him in Canada, and Lori just looked at me like, *Okaayy*, and I was like, *What?* And she goes, *Mail* it to him? Are you feeling OK? And I was like, Well you said you put it in an envelope, so I just figured you were going to send it to him.

She just gave me this total look and was like, I don't *think* so— are you, like, mental? Then he'd know I had it, and he'd think I, like, *wanted* it or something. God, Jenny, I can't even believe you just said that! Plus, it's not that kind of envelope, it's one of those little wax-paper ones from the orthodontist, you know, that your rubber bands come in? God, though, Jenny, I still can't believe you just said that. I swear, sometimes I think you are seriously mental. She sat there staring at me with her mouth open.

I was like, Well excuse me for living on planet earth—but I didn't say anything. I was just like, Whatever. Because that's the whole thing about Lori, she never lets anything drop. It's just like the nipple, it's like, no matter how small or totally irrelevant a thing is, if she's there, forget it, she'll get ahold of it somehow and keep bringing it up for all eternity. She's like if you had to look into one of those lit-up Revlon magnifying mirrors that make your face look like a mountainous terrain for like twenty-four hours a day.

And, incidentally, I know I'm not the only person who feels that way because for like six months after that, every time Meghan passed Lori in the hall, she'd wave her fingers in Lori's face like she was doing voodoo or trying to hypnotize her or something and go, *Woo, delighted, delighted.* So Lori basically stopped talking to Meghan altogether, but the whole thing about Meghan is that ever since the whole thing with the minister at her church hitting on her, she doesn't exactly care.

Aeneas Leaves Kansas

Amy Knox Brown

I will tell you, then, of my husband, a man who loved guns, who spent hours stroking an old petticoat along the barrel of his shotgun until it gleamed coldly, like the moon in December. Even then he might have been imagining the petticoat's ruffles were the foam of waves curving their way into shore.

Some saw in his silence a man of singular virtue, strong will. I saw in his silence an absence. A longing in him that the great fields of wheat dying in the drought tindered, as did the sound of the locusts that descended in punishment for what sin I don't know. That morning in August, I first thought the dark cloud moving toward us brought rain, but instead insects fell from the sky. We gathered the boys; we boarded the windows and closed ourselves in the house. Still, all night their grinding jaws chewed through the darkness.

I heard that people went mad from the sounds. I heard that some fool of a woman went out to the dead wheat to drive them away. Those locusts devoured the clothes off her body and left her to stumble naked back to the house, her body streaked brown with their spit.

Two days later, we woke to silence. The wheat had been eaten down to the ground. The sun blazed on a land that was nothing but dirt. The harvest is past, the summer is ended, and we are not saved. My husband packed his guns in the buggy, hitched up the mare, and said he'd send for us when he could. He didn't say where he was headed.

In town, the talk went that he'd been lured away by some woman, a *goddess*. I turned a deaf ear; I had my own explanation.

How often had he talked in his sleep, repeating the word *shore* over and over. I figured he'd gone east or west, drawn by the water.

The boys have stayed here, tied to the plow. I waited and wait. The seasons shift; the horses grow gray around their muzzles. Every spring arrives greener than the one before, and in those balmy days I think: Surely he'll return. From the front porch of our house, I look over the furrowed fields, those raised rows of earth. See that, I'd tell him if he were here. Don't they look like waves?

hey brother

Bekah Brunstetter

If he dies Over There, you will have something to write about. You will have some complex understanding of death, beyond Dave Eggers's books and obscure paintings hung in the Guggenheim. You will thank him for this gift of Content—Real Human Stuff— with a long posthumous poem written in the dark of your room. You will show up drunk at his funeral.

Before he Goes, fly home for the weekend. You can't afford it, so put it on your credit card. Tell everyone why you are going. Make sure everyone knows. Keep your eyes lowered while you say, *It's my last chance to see him, so. Yeah, I think he'll be fine. He's a really good shot.*

Ask him to pick you up from the airport. He can't, he's got things to do and doesn't want to drive all the way out There. But tell everyone that he is, for effect. In the car, ask Mom how he's doing, appear interested, but want a cigarette, want Chick-fil-A, want to go somewhere by yourself and do self things.

At home, find him downstairs on the couch watching *Arrested Development*, sprawled out like a giant Little Boy. *Hey, Brother*, use that voice he likes, it makes him laugh. Laugh together. *How you doing, are you good?* Search for fear in his eyes. You have never truly felt fear, so it'd be fun to see it. Nothing. He's laughing at the schmucks on TV, so just let him. Make him a sandwich with the Good Cheese. Bring him a beer. Scratch the top of his buzzed head for a few moments and stop just before it gets awkward. He has no questions for you, so you talk anyway. *Are you nervous, brother? Nah*, he burps. *I'm a really good shot.*

It's Saturday night, so take him out for a drink, go to That Bar where you won't see anyone from high school. It's too preppy and well lit. Offer to drive so he can have a good time. Get him drunk. Get drunk together, just a little bit. Feel proud to sit with him like you've got a puppy, a thing to show. Get him so drunk that he reminisces about when you shared bunk beds and how weird that was. When he's drunk, it's like you're pals. Discuss how chubby he used to be, and how chubby you Now are; how much he's grown. Actively listen. Attempt to know him, begin to write his eulogy in your mind. What are the heart-wrenching specifics? Try to hide your wide eyes when he reveals that he's set it up so that if he gets Killed, you get $100,000 so you can pay off your Student Loans. Watch him take a call from some bitch who's trying to make out with him, who wants to be his last before he goes. Pretend you're not hurt when he wants to leave, can you drop him off at this party? *A lot of people there, might be fun, I don't know, might be fun.* Of course you can, and you will, so you do. Don't wreck the car on the way home, don't get a DUI, though that would be funny and something to Write about.

Sunday Morning, stand next to him and his hangover at church. He's wearing his uniform for fun, you guess, and your dress is wrinkled and inappropriate. Sing these words, this hymn, because everyone else is doing it: *No Guilt in Life, No Fear in Death, Jesus controls my Destiny.* Watch him sing these words, does he mean it? Do you? Does anyone? Don't be so judgmental of the pastor when he, grandiose, announces your Brother's imminent departure. He is probably a very nice man.

Before you Go, make him a cake, goddamnit, it's the least you can do, it's one of the few things you're really good at. Stop at Harris Teeter on the way home from church for colored icing. Scrutinize the choice of colors, the flavor of the thing, what would he like best? Fuck up the "S" of "Semper Fi" and spend twenty minutes rectifying the situation with a toothpick. Make it perfect. Make everyone eat it and toast him with apple juice. Before you go, hug him hard. *Bye, Brother.*

While he is Over There, stay dedicated to the ironic sporting of shrunken Marine Corps T-shirts. Over-watch the news. Every time your phone rings, drop the pan containing the pointless egg you

31

are frying in butter, feel your heart move to your teeth. Pray like you mean it, like Christmas, like a little kid, like a chant, *Dear Jesus, please keep him safeplease keep him safesafesafesafesafe.*

And maybe he does come back safe. Taller, tanner, leaner. You will Fly home even though you can't Afford it and you will hug him hard. There will be a Welcome Back Cake, there will be stories and drinks. He will have things to say about sand and guns and shit food from cans. You will attempt, again, to know him. *Hey Brother. Welcome back, dumbass. Let's hang out.*

But if he dies Over There, if you are then a Sister of a Dead Thing, you will probably not mourn in private, no sir. You will make a spectacle of Him and It and Yourself. Your black dress will be a ball gown and you'll wallow in it. You will write his story hard and good, you will say something true. You will become Famous because of it. It will be the thing you have to Say. *With what fervor and truth she depicts the great loss; her personal loss, and that of the country!* They'll say. *A bold new voice!*

But he will be Dead, and that will keep you up at night in your big new bed, in your one-bedroom apartment that you can afford all by yourself. You'll wake up to Him standing by the window with a Beer and a Hole through his Head, just wanting to talk.

Very Bad Children

Orson Scott Card

The Emperor of the Air left the grassy meadow of his throne room and walked across the pond, not wetting his feet, for he did not choose to experience the pleasures of the world again right now, when he had just realized that he was going to leave it.

He walked across the pond of his throne room, and because he was dying, he saw that he was also walking across a downtown plaza in a city that he recognized as Portland, Oregon, and young children who wanted desperately to appear strong and dangerous and tough were riding skateboards illegally up and down the broad steps of the plaza. They were so deft, these children, but they were, after all, playing a child's game, for all their strutting and posing as Very Bad Children.

It happened that these children were unseers, so they were unaware of the Emperor of the Air as he reached out and touched the crown of the head of the one with his long hair wound up inside his dirty red bandanna; he did not know that there should be a harmonica there, where the fingers of the Emperor of the Air touched him.

"Oh dancer," said the Emperor of the Air, "I bless you with a crown of music. All songs will shine from you, bright as the sun."

When he let go of the boy, not a fragment of a second had passed; only a seer would have known what the Emperor of the Air had done and said. The boy did not know. But as he reached the top of the broad steps, dancing his way upward, he let out a whoop of joy that drew the eyes of everyone in the plaza, for it was his song of triumph; and though the pinnacle was nothing much, the effort it had taken him to reach it was great, and so the song put a smile on the lips of all the adults who saw him. It was the song of childhood, and it woke their best memories—though for many of them,

33

those memories were not their own. They had been borrowed from stories of other childhoods better than the ones they actually lived. But wherever the memories came from, they had them, and treasured them, and the song of the red-bandannaed boy on his skateboard found that dear memory and made it shine.

To the seers on the plaza, though, the song was not just an inchoate cry. It had words. Here is the song the boy sang, without knowing he sang it:

I am alive and I am young.
I am stronger than you, and more skilled.
I am full of seed, but have no idea of what to do with it
So I have worked to make this skateboard obey me.
It takes me where I command it to go.
It is my flying carpet, for I am full of magic.

Look at it.
Look where I have taken it.
Look where it has taken me.
Is it not a pleasure to ride my skateboard?
Do you not wish you could ride with me?
Ride with me and I will take you through the air
Through the Empire of the Air.

For I have been chosen to sing
By the Emperor of the Air.
I am the chosen one.
He has anointed my head.
Ah, my bandanna is red.
It is the color of loud music.
It is the color of joyful noise.
I insist that you hear my song.
I insist that someone ride with me
Upon my skateboard.

Then, his song finished, he pushed off from the ground and skated longways down the gentle slope of the stairs and began to skip step to step, up a step, down a step.

34

Three girls saw the red-bandannaed boy, and the Emperor of the Air saw them see him. All three of them looked at the boy with a sneer, which was meant to say, We are not impressed, oh boy, not even by your song. We have our own song.

The Emperor of the Air came to these girls and touched them, all three of them, and here is what he said to them: "Oh ye three lovely daughters of men, I fill you up as a well fills with water, endlessly full no matter how much is drawn from you. It is the water of life ye have inside you. Love no man who does not know its worth."

And for the moment that the arms of the Emperor of the Air embraced them, the three girls paused and the sneers faded from their faces and they felt their own beauty and their own fullness, and the three of them whispered, not hearing each other, yet waiting for each to finish her phrase before answering with the next:

1: I am full.
2: I spill over.
3: A river flows from me.

1: I am alone.
2: Will no one sail upon my water
3: And find the source?

1: Throw no coins in this well.
2: Make no wishes.
3: Only drink.

1: For you
2: I will never
3: Run dry.

Then the Emperor of the Air took his arms from around the girls, and they looked at each other in surprise and laughed for reasons they could not fathom. But it was no longer the laughter of ridicule for the bold-singing boy in the red bandanna. It was now the laughter of water over clean stones, water spilling from deep cold pure places in the heart of the Earth.

....

January

Fred Chappell

This wasn't as long ago as it seems. My sister was three years old and she was following me to the barn. It was very cold. When the wind blew it hurt, but there was not much wind. It hurt too when I walked fast, the cold air cutting my lungs as I breathed more deeply, and so I walked slowly.

Step for step behind my sister whimpered. She wore only a little dress with puffy sleeves smothered in a thin blue sweater. She had long blond curls, and I thought they were brittle because it was so cold and might splinter on her shoulders like golden icicles. It was late dusk and the moon was yellow, bulgy and low over the hills of the pasture, a soft handful of butter.

There were men in the barn I had never seen. They sat on sacks of crushed corn and cottonseed meal in the dimness. They looked mute and solid. Someone said, "That's a little girl behind him."

One of the men rose and approached slowly. He was tall, and his gray eyes came toward me in the dusk. His hair was blond but not as yellow as my sister's.

"Where are you from, boy?" he asked.

"Home."

"Is that your sister?"

"Yes. She's Sandra. My name is James."

"Don't she have something more than that to wear?"

"I told her not to come with me."

"You better strike out," he said. "She'll freeze to death out here."

"Strike out?"

"You better light out for home." He rubbed his big wrists. "Hurry up and go on before she freezes to death."

"Come on," I told her. She was still whimpering. Her hands were scarlet, smaller and fatter than mine. I touched her hand with my finger and it felt like paper. There were small tears in her eyes, but her face was scared, not crying.

I started back. The rocks upon the road were cold. Once I didn't hear her whimpering and I looked and she was sitting in the road. In the dim light she looked far away. I went to her and took her elbows and made her stand up. "Come on," I said reproachfully, "you'll freeze to death."

We went on, but then she saw a great log beside the road and went to it and sat. She had stopped whimpering, but her eyes had become larger. They seemed as large as eggs. "Please come on," I said. "You'll freeze to death out here."

She looked up at me. I pulled at her. Her wrists felt glassy under my fingers. "What are you doing?" I cried. "Why won't you come on? You'll freeze to death." I couldn't move her. It terrified me because I thought she had frozen to the log.

It had got darker and the moon was larger.

I jerked her again and again, but she didn't get up. Nothing moved in her face. Two small tears were yet at the corner of each eye. She looked queer, stonelike, under the moonlight, and I thought something terrible had happened to her.

"What are you doing to her? Why don't you leave her alone?"

My father suddenly appeared behind me, huge and black in the moonlight. He too had a small tear in each eye. He was breathing heavily in a big jacket. White plumes of breath bannered in the air.

"What makes you hurt her? What gets into you?"

She raised her arms, and he gathered her to his jacket, holding her in both arms as in a nest. She knotted herself against his big chest, curling spontaneously.

He turned his back toward the moon and strode. Sometimes I had to trot to keep up, and I continued in the limping pace until we reached home.

"Open the door," my father said hoarsely.

My mother stood waiting inside and looked through my head at

37

my sister, red in my father's arms. "What happened?" she asked. Her mouth thinned.

I went to the brown stove and put my hand flat against its side, and it seemed a long time before its heat burned me. My face began to tickle.

"What were they doing?"

I walked to the window and looked at the moon huge and yellow behind the skinny maple branches. A dim spot emerged from the window pane as I breathed, and as I stood there it got larger and larger, like a gray flower unfolding, until it obscured the total moon.

where Love is

Kelly Cherry

I was packing to return to Wisconsin. Clothes spilled over every chair, like a weird new trend in interior decorating—the Laura Trashly look!—and books and papers occupied every surface-inch of table.

That left the floor for me and my suitcases, and for my earrings, which were in a small white cardboard box, a box that one of the larger, danglier pairs had originally come in.

A friend stopped by to see me. I had not heard from this friend in many years, and as I sat on the floor, groggy from a whole string of late nights of packing, I became mesmerized by the story of his recent life. He believed, actually believed, in survivalism. He planned to hide out in the hills and when the rest of the world had destroyed itself he would reemerge, strong and healthy from living on fruits and vegetables—and skinned possum and potato roots—to take control of what was left.

I imagined that the hills were not alive with the sound of music but were filled with hundreds of frightened men, men who had persuaded themselves that success would, still, come to them, if only they could wait till everyone else had come a cropper and failed. I saw hordes of wild men in store-bought army fatigues. They were roaming the hills, foraging for food, occasionally raiding a nearby farm, perhaps reading Robert Bly. When the sun went down, they slept in separate caves, each man alone and dreaming.

While my visitor was talking and I was listening, my little dog chewed through the white cardboard box and ate all my earrings.

I didn't realize what my dog had done until almost midnight, long after my visitor had left. Worried about my little dog—*could he get food poisoning from an earring? puncture his little insides on an*

39

earring post?—I called the vet. "Take him for a walk in the morning," said the vet, "and see what comes out."

The sun gleamed like a gold hoop earring as we set out. In a few minutes, my dog had stopped to commune with a patch of earth. Sure enough, there was one of the rhinestone earrings, and here were both of the heart-shaped green ones, and here was an intricately wrought East Indian earring purchased in the East Village and there was its mate. Perhaps the earrings were a bit worse for the wear and tear, but my little dog was fine.

So we walked along, with me using a twig to fish around and a Baggie to stow my catch. By the time we finished our walk, nearly all the earrings had put in an appearance.

I washed them, and later that summer my father, amused by the incident and delighted to be of help, volunteered to sterilize them. He transferred the sterilized earrings to a new container, which he labeled, in handwriting, "Nina's Earrings," as if next time my dog might read the label and be deterred from eating them. But I never wore them again.

All the same, I never could throw them out. They had traveled through my dog's body, and my father's hands, and that made them more than just mine. The label should have read "Nina's and Her Dog's and Her Father's Earrings." They were no longer mine to throw away.

I think, sometimes, about the survivalist. I think we survive, if we survive, not by taking to the hills and feeding on what's there, unprocessed, but by being processed. Something swallows us and we make a long, dark journey at the end—the end!—of which we are still here, shiny and scintillating, bright as treasure, diamonds in the roughage.

I don't know what has become of the survivalist, but my father has died—that generous, self-denying man—and my little dog is no longer a puppy.

Yeats wrote,

Love has pitched his mansion in
The place of excrement.

And this is very true.

A Way in a Manger

Elizabeth Cox

On the night of the Christmas play given by the Hope Valley School third-graders, rain came down hard and the children wished it were snow, though in Tennessee they rarely saw the spectacle of snow.

"It'll snow, I bet," Johnny Johnson said. Johnny was the tallest boy in class, and he could run faster than any boy in the third or fourth grade. In fact, he seemed always to be running.

"You always say that, but it never does," Heather said. Heather Milton had been chosen to play Mary because of her long dark hair and brown eyes. She was petite but feisty, and usually objected in a loud voice. She didn't want to play Mary. "I hate Mary. I always have to be Mary. I want to be a Shepherd or a King."

"You can't. You're a girl," said William Raney, who was the class clown but rowdy, loud, troublesome, and inclined to curse freely.

"A girl can be a King," Annie Bateman said. Annie, with her blond mop of curls, was a tomboy and good at every sport she played. She liked to hang out with William and curse.

The first day of play practice had started with nobody wanting to be the character they had been assigned. Mrs. Bordwell, an older woman, staunch with confidence, had put on the same play for twenty-two years. But children nowadays were less willing to follow instructions. They were less content to be told what to do or be given lines to speak.

William Raney, for instance, wanted to be a cow. He had been a cow in second grade, and second-graders didn't have lines to memorize. He objected when Mrs. Bordwell refused.

"You did that last year." She tried to inspire him. "You're older now. You need a more responsible role."

41

"I hate re-spon-sible," William said. It was true. He did.

Fergus sidled up to William. Fergus Golchek, from Poland, could speak words in a foreign language. Sometimes he taught those words to William, who used them when he wanted to curse.

They had been fighting Mrs. Bordwell for five weeks, Johnny, William, Annie, Fergus, and Heather. Annie and Heather fought over whose doll would be in the manger. Annie's doll had been chosen, but Heather, living with her grandmother, had recently received a doll from her parents, who were traveling in Europe. She wanted her doll to have a special place in the manger. Finally, Mrs. Bordwell said *both* dolls could be in the manger, as long as the audience couldn't see *two* babies.

"Twins," Annie said.

"That would be difficult to explain," Mrs. Bordwell said.

"Dif-fi-cult." Fergus liked to repeat what people said, and the habit drove everybody crazy. The principal spoke to Mr. Golchek about the problem, and Mr. Golchek said, "I don't know why Fergus not behaf and say those wards. He not behaf like that for may." Fergus had five brothers and sisters—all younger than himself.

Tonight, the second-graders wore animal costumes and stood on all fours near bales of hay. A large cardboard tree stood near the open barn door, made from a wide plank covered in aluminum foil. Clumps of hay lay scattered over the stage, and Annie threw pieces at William. William told her, "Stop, damn it." He felt nervous about saying his lines. He didn't want to forget them in front of everybody. He was one of the Three Kings bearing gifts and had to say, "We have brought frankincense and myrrh." No one would tell him what either of those things were. He kept saying his lines aloud to himself.

"Myrrh," said Fergus.

Mrs. Bordwell held up her hands. They could hear the hum of the audience. Annie had peeked to see where her parents were sitting. Their divorce was not yet final, and Annie did not know which parent she would be with on Christmas Day. Her mother sat in the second row, as promised. She looked wooden and alone. Her father sat on the far left with Annie's big brother, Paul.

Mrs. Bordwell beamed with anticipation and said she was sure everyone would do well. The children grew quiet. The curtain was about to open. Suddenly one second-grader complained about being a cow, and Mrs. Bordwell quickly had him switch costumes with a sheep.

The crowd had settled. William's father and his two brothers sat near the back of the room. His mother was not there. She had not been around for a year. Everyone explained her absence merely by saying that she "was away for a while." No one would tell William where she had gone.

Heather's grandmother sat on the end of a row, her cane propped beside her. Sometimes her oldness embarrassed Heather. Heather had lived with her grandmother for the last ten months while her parents traveled.

Fergus had told his parents not to come, but they were there, in the back row. His father was standing. A proud man. Mr. Golchek had a thick accent, which the other children made fun of. Fergus had no accent at all, though at times he showed his father's difficulty with pronunciation, and the children sometimes laughed.

Johnny's mother sat in the first row in a wheelchair. She was always in a wheelchair. She looked withered from the waist down. His father sat beside her, hovering. Johnny was an only child.

Mrs. Bordwell shushed the children and told them to try to look "reverent." William asked what that meant.

"It means you are thinking about God," said Mrs. Bordwell. "God loves you no matter what happens." She seemed now to be remembering something in her own life. "No matter what, God's love," and she pointed to the manger with two dolls, "is always there."

The children nodded, thoughtfully: the Shepherds and Three Wise Men, Mary, Joseph, the Inn Keeper, the Kings, all the cows and sheep. A soft light shone down on the manger, and they all turned to see it, wanting to see what God's love looked like. Annie Bateman, dressed as a King with a crown sitting precariously on top of her curls, stood beside William Raney. Before the curtain opened, she leaned toward the manger and removed her own doll, pitching it to someone offstage. Heather nodded to Annie and turned back toward the manger. Outside, a light snow began to fall, but they would not know this until the play was over.

Mrs. Bordwell wore a navy blue dress with a wide belt that went around a substantial waistline. She announced the performance, then walked to the piano and began to play "Silent Night." The first-graders sang raggedly, as the heavy curtain rose to reveal each child in costume before the dark space of the audience. The uneasy air between the children and those sitting in the auditorium seemed enormous, but the yellow light on the stage shimmered. Each family grew still as trees, and the smell of hay offered an earthy context to the moment.

After the song, Johnny, a Wise Man, began to speak his lines. He pointed to the tinfoil Star in the East, which hung lopsided from a wire made of coat hangers.

"Behold, the star," he said, keeping his arm in the air, "stopping over the place where the child sleeps!"

Heather, sitting at the manger, waved to her grandmother, who leaned forward trying to hear.

Annie's mother was crying softly in the second row when Annie, standing very straight-backed, said her own line.

"We have come with our offerings," Annie roared.

"Off-fer-ings," Fergus chanted from the edge of the barn door. He was a Shepherd and held his staff at an angle. Mrs. Bordwell shushed him loudly. Fergus looked embarrassed, but his own line was coming next.

"We were biding our sheep in the fields," Fergus said bravely, "when the Angel of the Lord spoke and said, 'Lo' . . ." But he panicked, not remembering the rest of his line.

In the far back of the room Mr. Golchek, still standing, spoke clearly into the awkward waiting.

"Ah chall es bo-arn," he said.

"A child is born," said Fergus.

All of the audience clapped. The children looked up, their faces a slate of expectation and uncertainty. Fergus smiled, nodding to Mrs. Bordwell in the wings. She clasped her hands together in praise. When the clapping stopped, the room grew quiet for a long moment—a frothy silence breaking through the space of dark air, like the head of a small white flower barely above ground.

small

Quinn Dalton

Roy's not. But the word's out on his box, and now they call him *li'l bit* at school. He thought he could deal, but then Hector—*his friend*—called it a dollhouse, and Roy blanked after *take it back*, and now Hector's got a cracked rib and a busted eardrum, and after that it doesn't matter that last summer Roy carried Hector's little brother up eight flights of steps to their mama when he cut his cheek open trying to clear a fire hydrant on his bike. Or that Hector and Roy go way back, staying in the same four-room cribs, just on different floors, the projects like fat square monsters up on the hill, gonna crush them.

Hector's mama called Roy a menace. Now Roy's mama got to get to the school after her nightwatch job and ask the principal can Roy come back. *Send me begging*, his mama say. *You want that?* She's down there now, and Roy's waiting.

Roy's brother Damen says motherfucker had it coming. Roy's sister Tamika says he better watch his crazy self if he wants to get anywhere in this life. She brought him the notebook, helped him make his house pictures look real. Perspective. Means things up close are large and things far away are small. And everything comes to a point. She wrote it in his notebook, and he copied it until it seemed like something he could say.

Wood crate came from a Dumpster. Roy sprayed it red, painted windows too with Wite-out he stole from Miz Fulson's desk. Inside, matchbox beds in all four bedrooms with dishrag bedspreads, everybody gets one. Pictures on the cardboard walls cut from magazines. One of Tamika's glitter earrings for a hanging lamp. Big-screen TV (old eye shadow box from his mama) in the living room.

46

Roy's looking, planning for what to add next, when his mama come in crying. Says he got to go to special ed. *For motional problems.*

Motional? Roy's got no problem with motion. He raises his arms straight out. He's flying over the house in a plane. He's seeing everybody in there now, happy. Everything small because it's so far away.

The True Daughter

Angela Davis-Gardner

This is what my mother told me, after the divorce:

During the time when she and my father were married and my brother and I were growing up, she was living a fantasy. She had an imagined family with whom she lived day after day, a husband who loved her, appreciative children. For all those years when she was cooking, planting hyacinths, driving me to swimming lessons and my brother to violin, we were living side by side with a shadow family.

There was another girl beside me, just out of sight. Now it seems that if I'd turned quickly enough I could have seen her, but it doesn't matter, I know her, I knew her then, this other girl who slept in my room. She rose to the alarm without complaint, helped with breakfast and washing up, walked down the hill on time for the school bus, confident, responsible, in her bookbag her home-work all in order, concatenations of 5 apples 7 oranges 8 pears on trains approaching in opposite directions at different speeds cleverly and neatly completed, the pages numbered and named, while I was still wildly searching for shoes, books, glasses, late, late, late, so that my mother, with no more protest than a sigh, had to take me to school, and all along the way perhaps thinking of the true daughter, already in homeroom at her desk, reviewing her books, such excellent posture, knees and ankles together, a pretty girl but not too pretty, not in the way that made men turn in the street; no, it was wholesomeness that made her attractive, and her sterling character, and she did not inspire in my father extraor-dinary love and rage; furthermore, she was an honor student, a girl scout, a home ec standout, and later a scholarship winner who wrote home from college every week and always remembered her mother's birthday, wasn't vain, didn't charge clothes for herself without permission, was shorter than I, brown-haired, brown-eyed like her mother, smaller breasts than mine, a reasonable figure, nothing to get worked up over, no salivation from men wielding jackhammers, boys cutting meat in delicatessens, a sensible girl, feet on the ground, no cause for alarm about pregnancies, alcohol, drugs, commitments to the psychiatric ward, no sit-ins or protest marches; but not dull either, mind you, a keen interest in birds, history, gardening, needlepoint, and the cathedrals of Paris, which she and her lawyer husband recently went to view on their twenty-fifth wedding anniversary and sent cards home to Mother and to their children who are such fine grandchildren, well raised, unspoiled, love their Granny, and when Mother is a little older, they've told her, this daughter and her lawyer husband, she is welcome at their grand house in Atlanta (near the Piedmont Driving Club; he's old money) where there is a separate apartment waiting just for her, tastefully furnished and spacious, bookcases, even a fireplace, and a sunny window for her violets.

The apartment is just in case Dad—the fantasy Dad—dies first. But he's still going strong, takes care of himself, you see, physically fit, never drinks, he's a handsome man, not as handsome perhaps as my real father, but handsome is as handsome does and this man is no philanderer, he cherishes Mother, has ever been kind, gentle, never made her cry; a domestic sort, he calls himself, a homebody, modest, conservative in dress, no bow ties or odd shoes, only four-in-hands and wingtips; mad about his wife, really, but in a private way, only in the sanctity of their bedroom where all is gentility, no unusual demands, no garter belts or hint of the cathouse ever. He's churchgoing, maybe a little more religion than she'd like, but she keeps this to herself, it makes him steady, a sober, astute man who never spoiled the daughter nor could he be taken in by her, and who had man-to-man talks with the son, on whom he's never used the belt but has always taught by his good example.

The imagined son is taller than the daughter, brawny, resolute; his chin is cleft. He's no sissy, in spite of hours closeted with the violin; no pansy as the psychologists predicted, and he was not ever locked in his room drawing pictures of a man being hanged, a man who closely resembled our real father. This son was an athlete early on, lifting weights, jumping rope like a little boxer, so that he was never the bullies' target and he could always stand up to his sister, who no longer had any cause to gloat for he had friends galore, always with a gang, the in-crowd, and by high school— where he lettered in football, basketball, and tennis—he was voted Most Popular and Most Likely to Succeed. He was smarter than the daughter too, by a long shot: IQ off the charts, straight As, honor roll; in college, dean's list, valedictorian, even a Rhodes Scholarship, if he'd chosen. But he's no pantywaist intellectual, no mealy-mouthed college professor, and though there was a time of indecision—so many talents, which route to take?—he did not need years of prolonged counseling but confided in his mother, who tactfully ventured few opinions but was glad, secretly—she knew it was the right thing because he was always drawn to helping others—when he decided on med school, and now he's a respected neurologist who travels all over creation giving papers and of course he insists on his mother having the finest medical care, Duke, Mayo, wherever she needs to be, he knows all the right men.

When Mother died, eleven years after the divorce, my brother was in rehab drying out. She and I were alone in the hospital room. Her eyes were closed; an IV dripped morphine into a bruised and withered arm. I sat beside her, watching her small, pinched face against the pillow, a woman I never knew, who never knew me. Finally I bent down and whispered the question I'd hoarded all these years: Was there nothing in me that you loved? Her eyes moved behind closed lids, but she did not speak, she could not, already she was moving down the dark river, in the process of becoming a shade, and I thought, as the light seeped from the room and our forms grew indistinct, that worse than any answer is never to ask the question, for after our long silence we were nothing to each other, only two solitary figures in an unfamiliar room.

Registry

Sarah Dessen

When Tom said he wanted to call off the wedding, the first thing I thought of were the gifts. They'd been coming for weeks now, arriving almost daily: place settings, shiny new ladles, perfect cassoulet dishes without a single chip. The sound of the UPS man dropping a box on our porch—thump—had become so familiar, it was like the beating of my own heart.

Which stopped, suddenly, when Tom looked at me across the breakfast table and said, "I just think things have moved too fast" and "This isn't what I expected" and, worst of all, "I just need some time to think." All of it so foreign to me that later, retelling the story, I had to bracket his words with my fingers, creating air quotes to make them separate, not real, tucked away in a box of their own.

We'd met in a cooking class. My mother, reader of women's magazines, had decided it was a good place for me, her bordering-on-spinster daughter, to Find A Man. Up until that point, food was of little importance to me, my diet consisting of meals for one: Cup of Soup, a pack of Ramen, a single Lean Cuisine. But our instructor, a loud, rumpled man with a penchant for scallions, insisted that food could be art. The first night, we took simple egg whites and whipped them into beautiful, foamy peaks. Tom's station was short a whisk. Mine had an extra. Our love began with utensils.

I fell for Tom and cooking at the same time. His own skills, even postclass, were passable at best, but he considered everything I made delicious. He especially loved exotic food, so I kept signing up for more instruction, working my way through all the specialties the night school offered. I learned to roast pheasant, pickled my own ginger, and special-ordered by mail a frozen springtail jellyfish, the meat of which was supposed to be the most tender and sweet you'd ever tasted. They were also poisonous: miss a step in the intricate filleting process, and the results could be lethal. Mine had just arrived when Tom announced he was moving out.

Wedding planning is like a force of nature. You're not supposed to stop it once it begins. And yet that was what I was expected to do. Cancel the band, the caterer, the flowers. Somehow explain to the priest that God hated me, so his services were no longer required. It was like retracing your steps but finding yourself more lost along the way, not less.

"They have to be returned," my mother said, surveying our dining room table, where I'd lovingly displayed each and every bit of our new kitchenware, sorted by category and color. So much potential! I imagined myself going back to my chipped Corelle plates, the mismatched gas station giveaway mugs, my worn placemats, stained with the spills of a thousand lonely dinners. My life before Tom, my better-late-than-never, who, in choosing me, quieted the clucking of elderly aunts, saved me from piecing out my life in dollar-store tablespoons.

But now he'd changed his mind, wanted nothing of me, only reluctantly agreeing to come over on a set date to iron out a few last details. He said, "I can't stay" and "Let's just be civilized about this." I offered to cook him a meal, thinking it was my best chance at changing his mind. Food had brought us together; maybe it could keep us there. I got, "Fine, but something quick and simple" and "Don't go to too much trouble."

I went through hundreds of recipes, even as the travel agent left increasingly concerned messages about our honeymoon tickets and my dress sat at the tailor's, halfway altered, part me, part no one. My friends, trying to help, arrived bearing boxes, packing tape, and note cards to write brief and polite explanations. When I ignored them, immersed in *The Joy of Cooking*, they adjourned to the kitchen. There, huddled around my coffeemaker, they spoke in hushed tones. There was, "This is just terrible" and "Has anyone suggested Prozac?" and "Maybe she can just keep them" and "No. You're only allowed to do that if the groom dies."

It was as if I could see these last four words, coming toward me. They circled the earthenware mixing bowls, slid down the custom pizza stone, then curled themselves inside my mini soufflé dishes, precious as jewels. As I stared at them, slowly, they became something I recognized. A small sea creature with a tail like a spring. Just then, from the porch, there was the sound of another gift arriving, like a defibrillator touching my chest. Thump.

. . . .

common wall

Pamela Duncan

People in my duplex have frequent sex. Or rather, the people in the other half of my duplex have frequent sex. I just listen, but it's not that I'm listening. I can't help hearing. The wall between our apartments is so thin I hear everything, even silence.

When I turn off the television at eleven o'clock, they're usually already in bed. I try to be very quiet so I won't disturb them. I brush my teeth quietly, spit quietly, rinse quietly. The only sound I make is not really me but my bathroom cabinet door squealing as I close it.

They're very enthusiastic. Ted grunts and Susan speaks. "Oh, oh, oh, oh, oh, oh, oh, oh, oh, oh," she says at least ten times, getting louder with each one, and with a final, "YESSSSSSSSSSSS!" at the end. I don't think she's faking it; she's too consistent. If she was faking it, she'd probably vary it more, like, "Yes, oh yes, OH, OH, OH, YES!" or something like that.

Of course, this doesn't happen every night. Some nights Susan works late at the hospital and is too tired. She tells Ted, "I'll make it up to you tomorrow night, babe." He can't wait for her to get home. Of course, his job at the bank isn't as demanding as her nursing job.

They moved in right after they got married, about six months ago. I like them much better than Barbara and Stanley, who lived there two tenants ago, just before the single man whose name I never knew because he was so quiet. Barbara and Stanley reminded me of my parents because they fought all the time. When I was fifteen, I got a television in my room and I didn't have to listen to my parents anymore, but Barbara and Stanley fought louder than television. Once Barbara even had the nerve to come over at ten o'clock at night to complain about how loud my TV was, when all I did was turn up the volume to give them some privacy. I said I was sorry and used my TV earphones for a while. I try to be a considerate neighbor.

Stanley used to hit the wall when he got mad. It was very disturbing, all that banging and screaming. Barbara had to take him to the emergency room once because he broke his hand, and afterward they came home and made up in bed. She felt sorry for him, that he loved her that much.

The next night they were at it again, though, and that time Stanley didn't hit the wall. He hit Barbara. I thought about calling the police when I heard her screaming, but I don't like to be nosy. The police came anyway, and the next day the landlord asked them to move out. He said he wanted a better class of tenants. Which he has with Susan and Ted. Except for sex and occasional parties, they are very quiet and considerate. They always invite me to their parties, but of course I don't go. I turn up my television loud enough to match the party noise, that way they don't have to feel guilty.

Sometimes, if there's nothing good on TV, I turn it off and listen to Susan and Ted talk while they make dinner together. She tells him about patients at the hospital, and he tells her stories about the other bank manager trainees. Once she was telling about an old man patient of hers who had died that day. She was very upset, and Ted said, "Oh, honey," when she started to cry. I could just see him holding her, comforting her. It was very sweet, that little silence. Then she hiccuped and they laughed. They laugh a lot over there.

Sometimes at night I lie in bed and stare at our common wall and imagine them over there asleep in each other's arms, peaceful and safe. Sometimes it even makes me cry, how happy they are.

island

Pam Durban

Because of the morphine, she slept day and night now, and he sat beside the bed that Hospice had brought, thinking of all the things he still needed to tell her, like how good he'd been at gigging flounder when he was a boy. Low tide was the time to go, he'd say, on a night when the moon was too new or too old to make a mirror of the tidal creeks, and a person with a flashlight could see all the way to the bottom, where the flounder burrowed into the mud. He would stand with his gig in the bow of his father's dented metal fishing boat that had once been green, and his brother would stand next to him and aim the light. When he saw a flounder, he struck, then tossed the fish over his shoulder, got ready to stab again. He and his brother took turns in the bow with the light and the gig while their father steered the boat from a seat in the stern and collected the fish and cheered for his sons. Every time a fish got tossed, blood rained down, so that by the time the tide turned and the creeks rose and the fish disappeared beneath the murky water, everyone in the boat was spattered with blood.

One night, there were so many flounder, one gig was not enough, but it was dangerous to work two gigs in a small boat, so his father came up with a plan. They'd leave the boy on one side of the island while his brother and father went around to the other. "Divide and conquer," their father said. Then he'd poked the boy's brother in the shoulder. "Help me remember him, will you?" He loved a practical joke. Earlier that year, in a shop that sold magic tricks, he'd bought a little pink rubber pig with a hole in the belly that a plug fit into, like a salt shaker. He'd catch a few flies and put them into the pig, then set it on the table before a meal. The first Sunday dinner that the pig appeared on the table, the boy saw one ear twitch, then the tail. He couldn't believe it, so he watched until it happened again before he said, "See that? It moved. Watch."

His father felt his forehead. "You're not getting delirious, are you, Cooch?" he said, and the rest of the family laughed and he'd laughed along with them. He liked to hear his father call him Cooch, it meant he was teasing him, having fun. The trouble was, he needed to tell her, his father didn't know when to stop. He'd teased the boy about the pig until tears had stood in his eyes and he'd started to believe that he might really *be* the only gullible fool in the whole reasonable world.

He needed to tell her how his father and brother had left him on his side of the island with his gig and his bucket, how they'd shoved the boat back into the surf and his father jumped in, his pants rolled up to his knees, legs flashing white in the dark. "Go get 'em, Cooch," he said, as he yanked the rope and started the outboard motor. "We'll be back." The boy walked over the dunes and found the creek and sloshed along it in his rubber boots, gig raised, scanning the bottom with the light his father had rigged for him, a kind of miner's lamp on an elastic band around the crown of a wide-brimmed canvas hat.

When the bucket was full, he carried it out onto the beach and squatted on the sand and watched the waves come in and waited for his father and brother to come back for him. He listened to the swish of surf, the rattle of palmettos, and overhead he saw the stars and the long gauzy brightness of the Milky Way. He waited and he listened but no one came, and whenever he closed his eyes he remembered the pink rubber pig on the white tablecloth at Sunday dinner and the way his father liked to tease people until they felt foolish for believing what they'd believed. So he kept his eyes open and thought about how leaving your son alone on an island at night was different from teasing him about a pink rubber pig on the Sunday dinner table. Sometimes, though, his father didn't seem to know the difference, and that frightened him.

Then the thought of himself as a person a father could forget had made him feel as small and insignificant as a shell you picked up and dropped when you got tired of carrying it. When he finally heard the motor and the sound of their voices coming toward him across the water, he ran up into the dunes and lay flat on the sand where he could see them, like a spy. He heard the prow of the boat rasp across the sand. "Cooch?" his father called. The boy didn't answer. "COOCH." A command. Not to come after that was defiance, but he needed to tell her how he'd kept from answering by making himself small and forgettable again. The beam from his father's flashlight swept the beach, paused at the bucket of fish, moved on. "Goddamnit, boy, where are you?" He let the ocean answer and the silence of the stars. He waited and he listened while his father called and called. He did not know what he was listening for, but when he heard in the man's voice that his father felt small and frightened too, he stood up and walked out of the dunes and said, "Here I am."

DURING THE WAR, he fought in New Guinea, the Philippines, right up to the brink of Japan. She was his wife by then, and she wrote to him every day. Folded inside her letters were drawings of the house they'd build when he came home and photographs of her, looking coy under a new hat, or squares of cloth cut with pinking shears from a dress she was making. *Take care of you for me*, she signed each letter, and he would read the words and look at the photographs and touch the cloth and try to do what she asked. Mostly, though, his life came down to watching and listening from a foxhole in the rain at night, and when the rain pattered on his helmet and dripped from it and slid down his neck, the old desolation returned. Then, one night, he heard someone coming, and he looked up into the kind, tired face of another soldier, and the rain dripped from his helmet too. "Got a hot meal for you, Lieutenant," he said. He needed to tell her how the soldier's face and the warm tin plate had come out of the darkness like a gift that he'd carried with him ever since that night, but she was beyond reach now, she would never hear all the things he needed to tell her.

He sat beside her bed until the nurse from Hospice said it was time to call the children, and when that was done, he sat by her bed again and thought about how he would soon be alone on this earth, and he felt small and forgotten again, and angry too, as though something else had been promised. The night before the children came, a sudden thunderstorm blew in. The wind rose and lightening struck all around, and the sound of the thunder was like the sound of the big guns on the navy ships, shelling the beach before a landing. When the power went out, he went to the closet and found the battery-powered lantern he kept there for emergencies. He switched on the light and sat with it beside her bed so that if she woke she wouldn't be frightened. But the morphine rocked her and she didn't wake.

In the morning, as he'd done every morning since they'd moved her to the bed in the corner, he went and stood where she could see him. This was the moment of the day he dreaded most. She would look at him and look at him, and then she would remember, though every day it seemed to take longer for her to know him, and he needed to tell her how much that frightened him. He needed to thank her for all those letters. But on the morning after the storm, her eyes were as bright and sly as the eyes of a child with a secret. "Who were you fighting last night?" she whispered. "You were really fighting them." Then she drifted off to sleep again.

His heart jumped, and the words flooded through him like warm oil. She was right about the fighting. All night, he'd been down in the foxhole; he'd been waiting on the beach, forgotten. And somehow she'd found him there and walked with him across that stretch of night, violence, abandonment, and fear, and for the length of that short journey, he wanted to tell her, they had not been alone.

Contact

Clyde Edgerton

Thursday night. The teenage boy sat in the ER waiting room, leaning back against the wall. His right arm rested in his lap, lifeless. The father sat, leaning forward, elbows on knees, looking straight ahead through round wire-rimmed glasses. He was a plumber.

The father said, "Tell the doctor what happened. I don't care." The son's mouth remained clamped shut, as it had been—in the presence of his father—since his father walked out of their house months earlier.

The father had been picking up the son once a week and taking him to Hardee's for supper. There, in a booth, the father had finally stopped asking questions after a month or so and he thought, Was the boy going to spend his whole life not speaking to his goddamn *daddy*? Where would *that* get him?

On this night, the father, having come for the son, pushed the son violently in the shop behind their house. The son tripped and fell hard against an old anvil.

The nurse came, called the son's name. The father followed along as they walked down the hall. Again he said, "You can tell them what happened. I don't care."

"What happened?" asked the doctor. "Tell him," said the father. The boy looked away, and the doctor looked to the father for an answer. "We're having some family problems," said the father.

Later, in a booth at Hardee's an elderly couple sat eating in silence as was their custom. The woman heard a strange sound from the next booth—a coughing, raspy singing: *Rock a bye baby, in the tree top. When the wind blows the cradle will rock. When the da da the da da da da.*

Reverb

Tracie Fellers

He was handsome. Projects boy. Ghetto boy. Hair parted and sectioned off in those twists a lot of them are wearing now, sort of like little knots all over his head. But neat. Striking. I was waiting at the stoplight, watching him through the window on my way to the interstate this afternoon; he was walking and they seemed to suit him, those twists. They seemed just right with his burnished-oak skin and cheekbones, Lord have mercy, high and honed, enough to shatter your heart.

He stayed on the sidewalk, walking north toward the sign that said Isaacson Homes, his leather jacket puffed out by a sudden gust of wind, looking tall and taut and toned in his loose but not baggy obscene jeans. He kept his eyes focused straight ahead, matching the single-mindedness of his stride. Purposeful. Maybe even a little menacing. But not pimpy, not sloppy. There was a rhythm to his steps like a pulse, something I could feel under my skin, drumming strong enough to force its way through my window. I shifted, my right foot pressing lightly on the brake, all at once aware of the friction of my control-top pantyhose against my crotch. I sucked in a breath as I turned my eyes to the stoplight, excited, embarrassed. He was less than half my age; he was K.T.'s age I'd bet, but still I looked back at him. I turned back to the stoplight, then back to him. Stoplight, him. Stoplight, him. Hoping to catch his eye, and praying I wouldn't at the same time.

When the light turned green, I pressed down hard on the gas, catching up to the projects boy then leaving him behind. Even when I was bearing down on the entry ramp for the highway, when he was nothing more than a speck in my rearview mirror, his rhythm still sounded in my ears.

At home, late, I pulled David down on me and we made love. It was fierce and fast, almost animalistic, like we wanted to leave each other bruised, bitten, battered. I've never been into rough stuff, not even when I was first married to Nathan and we were barely in our twenties and couldn't wait to get at each other every night, before the barriers that rose up between us made us turn our backs to each other. Tonight I ended up on top of David, imagining that his soft belly was hard under my fingertips, harder than his heavy thighs that supported me. Imagining myself closer to the way I used to be, the fluid arch of my back, that moment of catching my breath as I'd feel my breasts rise. David trembled when he came, and in the involuntary shudder that shot through me, I flashed back to that sensation in the car. The stoplight. The projects boy. The pantyhose. And I came too.

Afterward, David and I lay side by side, barely touching, both of us breathing hard, but especially him. "I don't know what got you all hot and bothered tonight," he gasped, wiping fat beads of sweat from his forehead. "But I liked it." His salty lips felt like sandpaper on mine when he kissed me good night, and his chest was still damp when I leaned into him and closed my eyes.

K.T. AVOIDED MY EYES when she walked into the kitchen, and for a moment I felt a twinge of guilt, afraid she'd heard David and me last night and I'd been found out. Like our roles had been reversed. That feeling's been striking me more and more since the divorce, since she's developed a figure, curves to go along with her height and her attitude. She's not a child anymore, and David is a permanent part of our lives now. She might not like it, but she had to accept it.

"You better hurry if you're going to eat before you go," I said from my seat at the table, my edginess making me more abrupt than I intended.

"Not hungry." She stopped in front of the window over the sink, and I could hear David's car backing out of the driveway, could imagine the look on her face as she watched it.

"At least have some juice then." I rearranged the sections of the paper, reached for David's coffee cup and my own, stood to take them to the sink.

K.T. was still looking out the window, her back to me. "You could do better," she said finally, her voice even and cold.

"I'm sick of this, K.T.," I said, clattering the cups in the sink, my voice rising without my wanting it to. "Sick to death of it. You won't even try to meet him halfway, to give him a chance."

She turned and looked me in the eye, her upper lip curled in eighteen-year-old contempt, the spitting image of her father. "Why should I?" she said, the flat harshness in her voice stinging me like a slap.

I'm not sure whether her words or the sound of the door slamming set it off. But the ringing in my ears lasted all the way across town.

I SAW ANOTHER ONE TODAY, this time when I turned onto my street, coming home from work. He was right in front of me, walking to a car parked across from my house, taller, bigger, heavier; more of a man than the burnished oak–skinned boy.

This one was the color of bittersweet baking chocolate, and he moved toward his car unhurriedly, sauntering toward its dark windows and shiny chrome wheels as if he had all the time in the world to get where he wanted to go. He didn't have those twists either; he barely had any hair on his head at all. I neared him on the street, slowing down. He pulled a tiny phone from his pocket, and right as he reached the door to his car, about to open it, he turned and looked dead at me with a knowing smile.

I pulled in the driveway behind K.T.'s car, a used Toyota that Nathan gave her for her sixteenth birthday, and through my rear-view mirror, I watched the boy with the shaved head and satisfied smile drive away. I hurried in the house, light-headed and just about out of breath once I climbed the stairs to K.T.'s room, where I stopped in front of the door. The smell of sweat and leather hung in the air, and I stood there for a long time, trying my best to hear something stir. I waited, straining to hear the rustle of sheets, the hushed, breathy murmur of K.T.'s voice on the phone. But the only thing that echoed in my ears was the beating of my heart.

63

Runners

Ben Fountain

Jerry Baldwin would sit with us in study hall sometimes. He didn't really belong, though he seemed to think he did, and we, or at least most of us, basically tolerated him, his monotone, his deadly dull earnestness, his obsession with arcane sports trivia. He was a football player, a middle-school lineman of some promise who'd stopped growing around ninth or tenth grade, which gave his bulk a vaguely pointless air. The rest of us were runners: cross country in the fall, track in the spring, and maybe an ounce of spare body fat among us. Our suburban cross country course went down Jerry's street; meets were Friday afternoons, football games were Friday nights, and after school on those days Jerry would fix himself a couple of pregame sandwiches and sit out on his front steps, eating and cheering us on as we ran by. Showing his school spirit, I guess, or whatever species of solidarity he felt toward us.

It wasn't mutual. We thought we were so much smarter than Jerry; we were certainly faster, and more sarcastic, and it shames me now to think how we treated him. During track season, he did shot put and discus, and his little brother would follow him around the infield during meets, solemnly carrying his big brother's gym bag and sweats. And that was another Baldwin joke, how this boy was such a dead-on miniature of Jerry: the same rhino plod, the fat thighs that rubbed together, the pale, blunt head so much like a big toe.

A few years later this boy was killed in front of their house. He was mowing the grass one day, and stepped out into the street just when a car came hurtling over the rise. We were in college by then; Jerry had gone to junior college to play football, still hoping, evidently, for that last growth spurt. I hadn't seen him since gradua-

64

tion, but on hearing of his brother's death, I tried in the way that we always do to put myself inside the tragedy; to imagine, if only approximately, how one might cope with the enormity of something like that.

I couldn't, of course. We never can. Years passed. I graduated from college and moved away, married, started a family of my own. I stopped running; too many injuries, too little time, though if you've ever run that way it never really leaves you. We would always come back for Christmas visits, and one cold, rainy day we were driving far out in the country, going to or coming from some family gathering. Up ahead I spotted a man running along the road. A maniac, obviously, one of the hardcore; even in my youth I'd never been that crazy, to take it so far out on such a brutal day. I glanced at him as we passed, an ex-runner's tic, and I'd settled back in my seat before it hit me: Jerry Baldwin. He was lean, all muscle and sinew, and taller than I remembered. The entire shape of his body had changed; there was only that pale, blunt face to know him by, but even that was transformed by the sense of distance about his eyes, which had the calm and focus, the fixed unthinkingness, of a man who's been running for a very long time.

Davey Terwilliger

Philip Gerard

Mrs. Terwilliger lay dying in her bedroom that summer, and we played baseball every day with her sons. Davey was going on twelve, a small, wiry, towheaded boy. His little brother Natty tagged along everywhere, a snot-nosed eight-year-old with permanently mussed dark hair and a slouchy walk, as if he were afraid to stand up straight, that maybe somebody might knock him down. He was lousy at baseball, but we always let him play anyway because of Davey.

Davey was usually captain of one team or another. He played shortstop and pitched sometimes and had a tight, hard swing.

He had no choice but to bring Natty along, since he couldn't just leave him at home. He packed Natty's lunch and bought him sodas from the gas station with his paper route money, and whenever Natty scraped his knee or stubbed his toe, Davey would fish a Bandaid out of his dungarees pocket and gently smooth it onto the wound and say, "Don't cry, little brother. I got you covered." His father was some kind of professor and kept erratic hours. I think Davey must have cooked all their meals, any meals that were cooked, that is.

Their mother had been no help to either boy in a long time—though I recall her in summers past leaning on the chain-link fence that separated our houses and chatting with my mother as she hung wash on the line. Then she started dying. It was a small subdivision, a neighborhood where people scolded each other's children and borrowed tools and waved at each other on the street. And talked about Mrs. Terwilliger dying mysteriously in her bedroom.

I remember it was a Thursday when it happened, because that

was the day we always got supplements to stuff into the newspapers we delivered from canvas sacks slung across one shoulder. We hated supplements—all that extra weight to carry. I had finished my route and we were eating supper when Mr. Polk, from up the street, came to the door. He spoke in low tones to my father. I heard him say, "Doctor's there" and "Poor woman won't last the night," and there was more that I didn't hear. My father turned to my mother and said, tiredly, "I have to help find him," and the two of them went out into the cloudy bright twilight.

"What's wrong?" I asked my mother.

"Mr. Terwilliger has gone off again."

The men of the neighborhood were hunting him like a posse. He did this from time to time—went off. Sometimes they found him in the woods without his clothes or prancing along the Baltimore Road in his bathrobe and slippers. The men hunted a long time, and it was after dark when they shined a flashlight in his eyes as he cowered in the Fitches' cellarway, sobbing his eyes out.

When they got him home, Davey and little Natty were gone. I knew where to find them. I pedaled through the woods path to the baseball diamond behind the school, and I remember how the moon lit up the path like a floodlamp. First I heard Natty bawling like a goat. He was sitting on the visitors bench wailing and snotting, hugging his knees to his chest, rocking. Davey stood backward in the batter's box. He flipped a ball up and then swung the bat and whacked the ball into the backstop. He did this over and over. Each time, the bat made a dull crack and the ball *zinged* into the chain-link and he muttered something as he retrieved the ball. I got closer, so close he almost hit me with the bat and I felt it whiff past my cheek. He didn't even know I was there. His eyes were furious, without tears. His arms and neck and face were coated in sweat and dust. He batted the ball into the mesh and stomped toward it, muttering, "When do I get to, when do I get to, when do I?"

The Thing

Marianne Gingher

"I'm glad you're reading again," his daughter said, picking up the volume of Yeats. "You found a large-print edition? Good for you."

"It needs to be louder. Where's the thing?" he asked, pointing at the television. The TV was old, a black-and-white model, and didn't have a remote.

"What thing?"

"You know. The thing that fits on the thing down there. It's always falling off."

"Falling off what, Dad?"

"Never mind. I see it." The piece he was looking for was about the size of a crowned checker. He tipped forward in his chair and retrieved the little knob from where it had rolled close to his slipper.

"Here," he said. "Will you put it back on?"

"Where does it go?"

"On the other thing," he said. "That thing on the control thing that's sticking out. See it?"

"You're holding a volume-control knob," his daughter said in her impatient schoolteacher's voice. "You want me to twist it back on that empty metal stem at the front of the TV."

"That's what I said."

"No, you weren't specific. It's a *knob*. It has a special *function*. Without your telling me, I might have thought it was a button that fell off a coat."

"But it's not a button, Josie."

"From where I'm sitting I can't tell what it is. You could be holding a black button or a piece of chocolate for all I know."

"Please," he said tiredly. "It's not a piece of chocolate."

"Nor is it just a 'thing,' Dad. A 'thing' is an abstraction. You hate abstraction. Try to say what you mean and you'll eliminate confusion. *Everyone's*, including your own."

He grunted and slowly extricated himself from the chair. He stood there watching the golfers on the screen take their sweet time with their putts.

"Here, give me 'the thing,'" Josie said indulgently and winked.

He walked past her and screwed the knob onto its little metal armature himself. Then he turned off the TV. He didn't really want to watch golf. Even turned loud it was too serene. There was something melancholy about how late afternoon shadows overtook the brilliant fairway, the sunlight flaming here and there rather hopelessly like fool's gold, the golfers in their pale windy clothes luxuriating in it, dumb as moths. There was too much poetry roaring in the trees. He'd only turned the television on in the first place so they wouldn't need words.

The Tale Teller

Gail Godwin

He could contain all of me though in those days I grew fast. He was a man of infinite capacities though he never left his chair. One day I climbed aboard and found it promising. I settled myself in the angle most mutually comfortable and there I remained. I was a willing passenger to the end. I was never bored. He always gave a little more than I could take, and he never repeated himself.

I think people worried about my welfare with him. They were afraid he would corrupt me. But his corruption was all the welfare I needed. Other children played jacks and hide-and-seek and went home to supper. His lap was my home. He rocked me to sleep against his shoulder with the reverberations of his strange, spare stories. Often we dozed exhausted together in our inhalations and our exhalations. His left temple pressed upon my crown. Sometimes we dreamed the same dream. His rule was never repeat anything. One of a kind only. He dreamed his part of the dream and I dreamed mine. Once I dreamed I was killing him and he woke dying and we wept into each other's eyes. We were happy together. He had to tell the stories I had to hear. Just those and no more. He never repeated himself and never told a story superfluous to our needs. I snuggled in the lonely place between his trunk and thighs, and his voice filled the greedy hollow of my ear. As soon as my body grew to accommodate him, I filled other voids.

He hit me once. It was when I looked out of the window. I saw it was a fine day and asked if we could leave the chair and go out for a walk. It was then that I learned of his restriction. He shouted it at me only once and hit me once across the mouth. I did nothing to stop the blood. He licked it away himself and slipped inside of me. He told the most perfect story yet about the two of us going for a Walk.

So we went on together in our chair. Nothing ever repeated. No limit to what we could do in one chair. Stories and filling the other's voids. Rocking and filling our own.

Let me tell you about the stories. I can't repeat them because I only heard them once. But I will try to convey their shape and we can build on that. Contrary to what you might think, his stories were limited. A limitless man telling deliberately limited stories. He cut them to essentials. Honed them down to the bone. There would be time enough for flesh later, he said. He couldn't be bothered with that. No time for adjectives or proper names. Prune all distracting appendages. Yet he made me ravenous by his constant holding back. With the flat of his language he arrested the growth of miracles, but not until you'd felt their sting. Turning and turning upon the point of pain. Probing the limits of the void. Leave the extenuations to others. I sat almost continuously, my legs wrapped round his trunk. My ankles hooked behind his broad back. Our foreheads pressed together. But infinite variation in the pattern of the rocking. Constant innovation in the finger tracings on the other's back. Never a repetition. Most of the time we kept our eyes closed while we joined at the probing point.

Once I asked him about his restriction. That was permitted. I could ask anything once and he would answer it. Contrary to what I had believed, he was not crippled, though now his legs were possibly useless. He said one day he simply sat down in the chair. I climbed up shortly after. Though he doubted whether my coming made any difference. He would have gone on telling stories even to the bare walls. One void was as good as another. His remark wounded. I said other voids can't do what I am doing now. It's all the same in the end, he said. Though his stern face was suffused with delight. Such contradictions kept me in the chair.

I might have gone on like this interminably if I had not looked out of the window again. I say again, but I did not repeat myself. The first time I had looked out with my left eye. This time his eyes

71

were closed. We were between stories. Wrapped in our mutual silence and probing the void. My left cheek pressed against his left cheek. My right eye free to wander. It wandered out the window. It was a fine day. Fields filled with flowers all repeating themselves endlessly. Same sky. Then I saw you coming along in the fields, one step much like the other and possibly the same. I wanted to go out for a walk but could not say it aloud again. I felt his eyelid flicker questioningly against my cheek. I was terrified lest he had overheard my blasphemous thought. We were so close, you see. I closed the guilty eye at once and snuggled by mistake into a position we had already used up. With a cry of disgust he ejected me from the chair. I lay cold and empty on the floor at his feet. I did make one serious attempt to scale his legs a second time, being careful not to repeat the movements of my former climb. But as my head crested the shield of his knee, one enraged blue eye locked with mine and Good-bye, he said. He never repeated himself.

I crawled out into the coveted sun, which now burns me quicker toward death, and you found me there. How strange I must have seemed to you. How pale and otherworldly this creature like yourself yet unlike, struggling into the harsh light. You were alone in your fields not expecting anybody. You were generous by nature. You covered me with flowers until my skin grew hardened to sun. I taught you how to kiss. Your kisses were all alike but had on the whole a calming action. For long, monotonous stretches of afternoon you massaged my useless legs till I could limp along beside you. We became companion-lovers in that field of flowers. Then one day I grew strong and less grateful and began to desire his intricate novelties again. I took you by the hand and drew you in until you desired them too. I corrupted you.

Now we pace the limits of our field like caged animals, your ear bent obsessively to me as I tell you how he plundered me first, leaving a hollow no one else can fill, and how no walk we take no matter how long or where we walk will measure up to his story of the Walk, which distilled all walks down to their essential desirability. Sometimes you weep and I lick away your tears. But it's just a variation of the time he licked away my blood. Anything we do now is an extenuation of the things he would only let us do once. Our future must be repetitions of his single themes. Yet I have found with you an unexpected consolation. Mutual suffering was a thing I never had with him. So we've outdistanced him there. Though he would call it flesh upon the bones of his essentials. No matter. It trails behind it the progeny of hope. That hitherto unarticulated vulgarity.

We'll go on collaborating. You and I. Refining and emending and developing and reiterating our one story. And sometimes decorating like the time you covered me in flowers. It's all we have, and so we'll go on. Our brave legs scissoring through the flowers. I'll tell it to you again and again, each time adding something new. The things you don't know will keep me going. Though I'm like him. The audience makes no difference to the telling. One void is as good as another. If you weren't here, I'd tell it to the flowers.

GOD BOX

Jim Grimsley

The man came in, sat down at the God box, and started to play. He put his hands inside the box and music began. Pretty music. Nice music. Nothing else happened.

The woman came in and sat down beside him. She pursed her lips. Not only would she be forced to share the box, she would also have to begin after him. She began to play the box with a furious tightness in her fists.

"You were supposed to call me," she said. "We were supposed to come here together."

"I got tired of waiting," he said, his fingers fidgeting. She had a tone in her voice and a look on her face that caused him to cringe away from her, his body making the shape of a parenthesis. He was afraid to look at her, so he looked just to the side of her.

"You should have called." After that she said nothing else and they played.

For a while the music was astounding. Coruscating over them in waves, harmonies, and high crests, their two playings blended in the box. They closed their eyes, arched their spines, and swayed, moving like the necks of what would later be called swans.

Out of the music arose a thing that grew to become the whole universe, a pulsing that sometimes died away to nothing and sometimes filled all the space around them as she and he played.

She stopped abruptly and stood and his playing faltered and the music thinned and faded. She lifted her chin and looked out the window, beyond everything else.

"I won't play with you again until you apologize," she said, and walked away, and closed the door quietly behind her.

A brief wind swept over him as he sat in front of the useless, empty box. Around him, the music they had created gave a thorough shudder and a vast unease swept through it. Bad things began to happen everywhere.

contempt

Virginia Holman

The women were in the kitchen, talking of somebody's marriage that was busting up. "It's such a shame. Just when all the kids are in school, just when it's getting easier, they fall apart," one of them said.

"Joel says he'd never divorce me, because of the kids," Sylvia said. She glanced at her husband. He was in the other room, on his third scotch, talking to a much older, steely-haired woman.

"SHE GETS AN MBA AND A JD and works a few hours a week at that Women's Center," he was telling the woman. "She could be making real money. Instead we hire a $25,000 a year nanny so Sylvia can go to yoga, chat with her organic Stepford wives friends at Trader Joe's, and take paper-making classes. She went to Stanford!" He snorted.

The silver-haired woman laughed and placed her hand on his sleeve. "It's nice to have choices," she said. "And very nice of you to indulge her."

Joel gazed at the soft lacy bosom peeking out of the woman's sapphire silk shirt. He wondered if they were real. Who cared, they looked like heaven. Sylvia only bought organic cotton underwear. When the housekeeper was on vacation, he folded them.

She was hell on help. She was hell on everybody. When their son Steven was struggling with his viola, he'd watched Sylvia instruct him, horrified when she'd taken the bow and whacked him over the head with it. "It was hardly enough to hurt him," she'd explained coolly, "but it got his attention."

Who the crap cared about the viola? Really. Whatever happened to playing in the woods, riding bikes with your buddies till you got lost? Why couldn't the kids be kids? Why did they have to hover or hire people to hover over their kids every minute?

Joel believed she was a good woman. He thought she was mostly faithful even though she refused to come back from her weeklong art workshop when he'd smashed his arm bicycling home from the gym one night and the surgeon inserted five screws. He had the nanny to watch the kids, he'd be OK, she reassured him.

Who had she become? He really had no idea about the shape of her days. When the kids were young, the nanny would come when she was supposed to be studying for her bar exam. But he'd spied her more than once outside the second-run cinema and never called her on it. He believed she was there alone. He knew that she flirted, maybe she'd kissed a few men after they were married, happily sloshed. He'd given into temptation only twice, but he knew how to set limits, and it had been early in their marriage when it happened. He'd never told her, even when the guilt ate at him and even later, when it dissolved. He'd felt sure she'd prefer it that way. Still, he was certain she'd never slept with another man, didn't have it in her for a full-scale affair—she was too much in love with herself.

He'd loved her passion when they met, her ambition, but now it seemed like an act. She was more diffuse, shapeless like those waistless linen tunics all the women wore this year like some suburban burka. She called herself a "stay-at-home mom," but, honestly, with a housekeeper and a nanny and a gardener, she wasn't really devoting herself to anyone. She was just marking time between errands.

God, he'd been nuts for her. She'd worn these sexy little things, even under her sweats. They couldn't keep their mouths off each other. Now, when he slid open her underwear drawer, it was filled with ten pairs of enormous cotton underpants. They looked like something you'd see flapping on a clothesline.

When had he gone from wanting to fuck her to just wanting to fuck? Since she was his wife, he fucked her by default.

THE CATERERS CAME AROUND WITH CRAB CANAPÉS, and the steely-haired woman reached across him to take one. She smelled fresh and crisp. Her perfume made his mouth water, reminded him of basil and cucumber. He saw her naked in a garden, younger. She looked at him and smiled, then looked down. He felt filled suddenly with scotch, the golden afternoon light, with her great tits and soft smile and her skin smelling like a summer night. He knew that he would get her number, call her later from his garage, when he took the dog out to hunch in the corner by the fence. He knew that she'd be waiting. He'd tell her at the start, he'd never leave his wife. He was too crazy about the kids. He'd never, ever, leave.

. . . .

where she sits

Randall Kenan

They were in the little dining room off the kitchen when he finally told her. He paced about, motioning with his hands.

She just sat there, staring down. Feeling nothing. Maybe. Or just plain tired.

"I can't do it anymore, Sandra," he said.

Sandra said nothing. Slowly, she moved her hand over the oil-cloth, steadying herself.

"I don't care what your family says about me," he said. "I don't care. I can't . . . I'm not . . . I've got to . . ."

She might have asked Dean about the children. But the idea that he would come up with some sleazy nonsense only made her feel a wave of nausea. Sandra put her head down.

Dean stopped behind her. She could feel the tension in the air; without seeing him, she knew he was clenching and unclenching and clenching his fists. He did that when he was angry. "Did you hear me? I'm leaving."

Sandra raised her head. "Then go."

He stood there for the amount of time it takes a frying egg to turn white and walked from the room.

Sandra reached out and caressed the table, and remembered. Not so much remembered as allowed a flood of images, past scents, past sights, to overtake her, fill the void she was now harboring. Each image evoked something like a feeling. So much took place in this room, upon this very surface. Not merely the food served, or the homework fretted over, or the cards played, or the beer spilled, or the puzzles arranged. Moments occurred right here. And now, in this instance of illusions shattered, of dreams wrecked and a heart frozen, these moments seemed to simmer before her, behind her eyes, and she could only hold onto them, to find some strength.

She had inherited this very table from her great-grandmother. Made of pine, by whom she did not know, it had been oiled, dented, dusted, polished, chipped, varnished, battered, peed upon, burned, broken, mended, hammered, nailed, or some such for decades. If it could feel, she knew she'd feel the way it felt now . . .

"Sandra? Damn it! . . . Where is my . . ."

The first true memory of her grandmother had been watching her across this expanse, on the other end, smiling and slicing with pride a piping hot blueberry pie. No, child, wait for it to cool. And so many mornings, days, nights, her mother at that same end: What you doing out so late? Sandra! An A in math! Now that's good. Girl, don't you ever raise your voice at me. I'll knock the taste out your mouth! You heard about Uncle William, didn't you? . . .

"Sandra, can't find my . . ."

As if he actually expected her to come in there and help him to pack, to leave; as if any of this fault rested on her shoulders; as if she was expected to go along to get along; as if she would be unreasonable to go into the kitchen, get a butcher's knife, and chop him into seventeen billion little pieces.

She ran her hand out against it again, against its smooth flatness, as if to absorb some of its stolid solidity.

Here, she served him his first taste of her cooking: catfish, greens, mashed potatoes, corn bread; here, she told her mother she was to wed the man who made her legs feel like overcooked spaghetti and her heart feel like butter. Here, where she tended him, listened to his tales of boring sales meetings and petty office feuds, and where he entertained his buddies (when not in front of the TV); here, where she fed and consoled and interrogated first one, then two daughters; here, where she slowly watched the shoals of her marriage erode, grain by grain.

Oh, if it could talk . . .

"Sandra." He stood in the door. She didn't want to look up at him. She had nothing to say.

"Good-bye."

She did not look up, as he turned, wordless, and walked down the hall. As the door clicked behind him, she held fast. He may go, but some things would remain. A part, a piece, a fixture, a witness. Even now.

Downtown

John Kessel

So at the end of the week I shut down my left brain, got charged, and told anyone who would listen that I was going Downtown.

"And who is it that's supposed to care?" the Group Average said.

"Certainly not you," I said, pulling on my weekend skin. GA and I used to be featured, and they still held it against me.

"What you gonna do down there?" the Duck asked. The Duck was puny and naïve.

"Tell me something I *ain't* gonna do," I shot back.

Well, that seemed to intrigue the Duck. "Can I come too?"

"It's a free domain," I said. "Long as you got your own charge."

We left the Group by the lockers and walked out of there. The sun was dying and on the horizon the murder trees were stirred by the offshore breeze. We walked up to the transit stop, plugged in, bought a couple of passages, and stood on the platform in the sultry evening waiting for the slip. Far down the slipway glowed the lights of the city.

"Will there be boys and girls there?" the Duck asked.

"You bet your feathers," I replied. "Ducks too."

When the slip drew up we settled in, and before we knew it we were stepping out into the colorful Calle Rosinante. Boys! Girls! Snakes! Metatron the Archangel, Available for 23 Amps! Ducks!

Hot jazz filled my right brain, singing Go! Go!, along with the Four Noble Truths:

Life sucks.
It sucks because you're stuck on things.

This can be remedied.

Fake left, fake right, go up the middle.

Just like Downtown to kill your buzz while pushing it. Stuck on things? I wasn't going to be stuck on anything tonight longer than it took me to drink it or smoke it or poke it. Remedy me no remedies.

First, food. We got some food. A CosmicBoy accosted us in front of the cheesetaurant. "You're outliers, right? For a very reasonable price, I can provide an interstellar experience."

"How much?" the Duck asked.

Before Cosmic could answer I put the bigger of my two hands— my pushing hand—on his chest. I pushed. "We aren't interested, Chaz. My friend may look like a Duck, but he wasn't fledged yesterday."

Cosmic sauntered off. "Why did you chase him away?" the Duck asked.

My right brain informed me that I regretted saying the Duck could come. Thanks, right brain. "Look, Duck, let's split up. I'll meet you back here at daybreak and a half."

His display feathers drooped, but he didn't protest.

So I had me a night and a day and a night. Various transactions were made, physical and psychological. Fluids were transferred. Charges were discharged. Frankly, I don't remember most of it.

What I do remember is waking in an alley between a tavern and a frothel. The Duck was leaning over me. He had lost most of his feathers; his downy cheeks made him look like a girl. Holy calamity—he *was* a girl.

"Duck?" I said groggily.

"The one and only," she replied. She levered herself under my arm and helped me to stand. My weekend skin was ruined. My right brain whirled. "Come on, Schmee," she said. "Time to slip home."

"I can't slip," I croaked. "I'm completely discharged."

"I'll take care of it."

We limped through the street. Downtown was just as bright and attractive as it had been when we arrived, in a completely meretricious sort of way. Meretricious. That was my left brain coming back.

We stood on the platform waiting for the slip. Ahead: another week in the reality mines. "Life sucks," I muttered.

"This can be remedied," the Duck said. To my utter and complete surprise, she kissed me on the cheek.

She is really quite attractive, for a duck.

· ·

I Dream

Haven Kimmel

Her name was Jean, but my best friend called herself Genie, and misspelled it. She had a boyfriend, Darrin, who drove a blue Chevy Nova with a white stripe down the hood. His eyes were narrow, too close together; his hair and ears and forehead were perfectly simian, and he was tall and thin. His belt was unbelievably too wide. Their romance was a mystery, although I tried to solve it by buying an issue of *True Romance* magazine and reading every word. I learned that if you want to develop a more appreciative relationship to sperm, you should have your boyfriend eat a lot of cinnamon. This advice was not helpful.

We were only fourteen, but Genie had had sex with Darrin upwards of five times. The most recent occasion had been at his house, on a Sunday, while his mother was at the grocery store. I didn't want to hear about it, but Genie insisted. She had been on top, she began, and then she proceeded to describe what that meant and how it felt. I knew she intended to sound romantic and reckless, but all I heard was something vaguely surgical and no more romantic than something I might have discovered at the back of our medicine cabinet.

On Saturday we put on our bathing suits, sprayed Sun-In on our hair, and lay out in the sunshine in lawn chairs. Genie's house was on the corner of a crossroads with no name and was surrounded by cornfields. Her garage was larger than her house, and her parents had lived there forty years. I didn't last long in the sun; I never lasted long in such an inexplicable situation. I did, however, manage to turn my hair into the same nightmarish shade Ronald McDonald sported and to burn my nose. I took a shower then lay on Genie's bed while she showered and dried her long blond hair, which had sun in it just right. I listened to Dr. Hook and read Judy Blume. Genie had glow-in-the-dark stars all over her ceiling and a collection of lip glosses in all flavors of soda. Her boyfriend was on his way over with a friend named Ricky.

When the boys arrived, Genie and I were wearing matching one-piece short outfits that were held up solely by elastic bands around our chests. They were terry cloth—hers was aqua blue and mine was cream. Her eyes were blue and mine were brown. Ricky turned out to be a hard rockin' dude, with long hair already thinning, a beard and a mustache, and a big belly. He was wearing a T-shirt from a Black Sabbath concert. I couldn't look at him, and I couldn't look at Genie and Darrin on the nubbly rose-colored sofa in the living room because Genie was in Darrin's lap again and her parents, who had had Genie late in life, were only outside in the garden. We were listening to a Meat Loaf album, and that also made me miserable because Ricky looked something like a meat loaf and if he burst into song I would have to kill myself. There was no place I could actually rest my eyeballs. Darrin pretended to be the baby from the movie It's Alive, and Ricky suggested we all go out for a walk.

We crossed the road and went into the field, which had been planted in grass for years. Sometimes Genie's neighbors kept horses, but there hadn't been one for a long time. I kept my distance from Ricky, who looked at me periodically out from under his rock 'n' roll forehead. When we got to the creek I couldn't help myself, and I turned to say to Genie that I thought the whole situation would make a very picturesque commercial—I had been noticing such scenes for a while, or perhaps I was simply overwhelmed with youthful irony—and saw that she and Darrin were locked in a hideous kiss. It was the sort of thing practiced by aliens and felons. I turned and ran down under the little bridge where Genie and I had spent many hours over the past five years. We had written poetry in chalk on the cement walls that led down into the water. We had caught crawdaddys and tried to cook them over an open fire. There was evidence of us everywhere down there: an empty Mountain Dew can, a broken pencil, a comb that must have slipped from my back pocket. I looked for crawdaddys but there were none. I thought how stupid I was. I wondered what was being said about me.

When I emerged from under the bridge, I found them, the other three, only about ten yards away. Ricky was holding a huge black snake just under the head, with his foot on the tail. He had the snake stretched out as far as it would go, and it appeared to be about five feet long. The boys were laughing, and Darrin had pulled out a pocketknife. I knew what was about to happen. Genie was standing only a few feet from her boyfriend, with her arms crossed over her chest. She knew, I knew, that black snakes were harmless, and no matter how many die, the population is never diminished. She turned and looked at me; her expression was flat; there was nothing in it I recognized. I headed back toward the house just as Darrin cut off the snake's head and tossed it in the air like a coin.

My Family

Carrie Knowles

Third grade: 1957. We read about being handicapped, and the teacher calls on me to explain what it is like having a blind father.

"Blindness isn't a handicap," I say.

"Of course it is," she insists.

I argue with her until I can no longer stand the horrible silence and the acrid taste of pity in the room.

I bolt, run to the door, through the playground, then all the way home. My mother is there, waiting for me.

It is the first time I realize that our family, not just my father, is different.

Keening . . . 1 Mile

Telisha Moore Leigg

"So, you really came," Mama said. The chipped, faded-white screen door separated us from Pop.

"Where are you taking her this time, Kain? When will you be back?" Pop shrugged, leaned, and looked at the worn welcome mat on the cracked cement porch, then at the weatherboard house.

"You could use a coat of paint here, Charlotte," Pop said. Mama's lips thinned, but she said nothing. Pop looked down to me and smiled.

"We're going to King's Dominion, ain't we Emma?" I nodded, my head full of roller coasters and cotton candy. Mama followed us off the porch steps carrying a Dr. Seuss book (I was only five) and a green sweater.

"Call me if you need anything, OK baby? Have her back by tomorrow morning." Mama went back into the house.

Pop opened the door of a blue four-door sedan and I got in. The seat was sun-warmed, and I noted the contrast of seats in this sedan and in Mama's old green Duster. These seats were new and uncracked. We drove out of my neighborhood and onto the highway in silence.

"Pop! Look Pop, I can read," I said opening my Dr. Seuss book. His eyes widened in surprise, and he listened for a while. He listened long enough to know I was only creating plots from pictures. I lost his attention. Silence resumed. We drove for a while, past service stations, cows, horses, lots of trees. Pop asked for the third time if I was sleepy. I said no and hoped the conversation would continue this time. He turned on the radio. Jazz, soft and moody, weighted the car.

I decided to prove myself (really to make up for my earlier

Dr. Seuss debacle) by reading road signs, the big green boards. Pop would be proud. At the first green board, I picked the top word, K-e-e . . . . . . , before it became a blur. I waited, scanning through the dashboard window, for the next green board.

Three gas stations and one tractor later, Pop pulled into this driveway and a tall, skinny black man got in. His army-green jacket was old and scratchy against me.

"Hey, Kain, ready to go fishing!"

Pop cut him a look and then jerked pointedly at me. It was only then that I noticed the tackle box and fishing rods in the back seat.

"We going fishing 'stead of King's Dominion?" I asked, tugging on Pop's sleeve.

". . . Ah, yeah baby."

I sat back between them, mollified. The trip progressed. Above me, they talked quietly. I saw my green board again, K-e-e-n (blur) . . . . 5. I was getting close to the end. Pop then took a left turn on some country road, barely paved and bumpy. It went on forever, unbroken past pine trees and wild grass bending like Indian women wailing.

Finally, we came to a fork in the road. The green board was back. I caught the end of my word. K-e-e-n-i-n-g . . . 1. My mind turned it over and over, trying it silently on my tongue. Kee-ning. Ke-ening. Keen-ing. Then something wonderful and sweet connected sound and memory and I understood. The word was Keening, as in Keening, Virginia. I hugged my secret. I wanted to smile, but something told me to wait.

The car turned onto a little red path, slightly graveled and rutted. At the end of the trail was a brown, rough-shingled house. I jerked on Pop's arm.

"Pop!" I said, already knowing there wasn't going to be any King's Dominion or fishing.

Kain didn't answer.

"This is . . . this is Grandma's!" meaning his mother's house. The word *Keening* rang in my head over and again. I felt stupid, angry, and betrayed by my ignorance and my intelligence. The green boards had said *Keening, Virginia*, all along. They said *Keening, Virginia*, where my father's mother lived, where I would be left until Pop returned from whatever he and the stranger would do without me. I cried, hugging my Dr. Seuss book and green sweater.

"Hush up, now. Go say hello to Grandma." The wrinkled black woman smiled at me. But I wouldn't get out of the car. I cried harder.

The sedan left me crying and sniveling in my grandmother's dirt yard. From inside the house, I heard Grandma speaking, "No. I don't know where Kain is, Charlotte. . . . Yes, she's crying. Come and get her." And Mama came and got me, in her old green Duster with the cracked seats, out of Keening, out of Keening, Virginia.

Hicks and Losers

Peter Makuck

"Dad, teach me how to shoot!"

Waiting for my son and his buddy to come off the Tilt-a-Whirl, I had heard the telltale crack and clank of a shooting gallery; it pulled me in. Remington pumps that fired .22 shorts. Easily 22 years. I wondered if I still had the old deadeye. No problem. Ducks fell and candles went out. When he found me, Mike was excited because he had no idea I knew how to shoot. But his fierce look upset me. Not long ago he had come home with a bloody nose and wanted me to teach him how to fight. He wanted to kill this kid on the school bus. His face was sad and ugly with tears: *I'd like to blow him away!*

"This isn't for kids," I said, putting the chained rifle back on the carpet-covered counter. The midway was all people, dust, and noise.

Mike yelled, "Dad, can I have a .22 for my birthday?"

Before turning away, I picked up one of the small shells and brought it to my nose. The scent of brass and odor of burnt powder made time dissolve.

LEE HUNG OUT WITH ME AND FRANK our last year in high school. He had an unshakable cool and a face that was all angles, with deep-set eyes. He was full of stories that usually had him in some starring role, like the time he tackled a guy at the neighborhood pharmacy. The guy had presented a forged prescription, then tried to run. Lee happened onto the scene and hammerlocked the guy until the cops arrived. The junkie's capture was in the newspaper but nothing about Lee. Lee's stories always had a germ of truth, but you doubted the heroic details, suspected, too, that he wasn't scoring with the cheerleaders he bragged about, even though you saw him schmoozing with them between classes. After one of Lee's stories, Frank said, "Man, he ought to forget about college. Just sell tickets to his dreams—he'd make a fortune."

Why he hung out with us was a mystery. I suspected slumming. His father was a doctor. But Lee's mother and Frank's mother went to the same church and lived in the same neighborhood. Anyway, Lee wasn't like us at all. Golf was his game. Frank and I were nutty about guns and cars. We hunted rabbits and pheasants and worked on cars at my father's service station. Lee didn't have a car. He had big words and liked to chuck them around. Sometimes he corrected Frank's grammar, winking at me on the sly.

I had a 1951 Merc and worked on it endlessly. Spotted with gray primer, frenched headlights, and electric doors, it was nothing to look at, but with the Olds Rocket V8 we shoehorned under the hood, she really stepped out. Lee was often at the garage too, but reading books and tuning the radio. Never got his hands dirty. At night, whenever we cruised the hot spots, Lee wanted to ride shotgun, but I wouldn't let him.

One night, for no apparent reason, a carload of guys from another town chased and cornered us on a dead-end street. We took a beating, and my car took a lot of jack-handle hits. With a final boot to my ribs, one of the guys said, "Man, you ought to keep your buddy in back there from flipping off strangers." Then I noticed that Lee had stayed in the car. His story was that my electric doors "malfunctioned" and he couldn't get out to help us. The fight cost Frank a trip to the dentist and cost me, besides my lumps and cuts, time and money to undent my fenders and replace a window.

Lee made himself scarce for a few weeks, but then he was back, all cool and control, mockery in his eyes and the kind of smirk our nuns would charge down the aisle to smack off your face. He said he had been boning up for college boards. He wanted to get out of this dump of a town, he said, a place, that was full of hicks and losers. I don't think he even realized what he said. But it was said. And I decided that one of the losers, Hoss King, ought to hear about Lee's imitations. Hoss was big and had an equine face. After hearing how Lee made him a figure of fun (nickering and hoofing answers to math problems), ol' Hoss would clean his whistle and, for once, I'd enjoy seeing Mr. Cool collapse. But something intervened.

One winter day, Frank and I decided to skip school and hunt for ringnecks. Frank's mother was making breakfast for his younger brother. The smell of frying bacon was wonderful when I stepped in from the cold. I said hello to Mrs. Cone and took the stairway just off the kitchen that led upstairs. Lee was there. Frank was pulling on boots, and his 16-gauge Savage lay across the bed. Lee picked up the gun and aimed it at me: "Go ahead, make one false move."

Frank grabbed the gun from Lee and said, "Let's go."

Lee said, "Man, I wish I could go with you guys, but I got too many cuts. Mr. Flanagan makes one more phone call home and I'm dead." More bullshit, but I said nothing.

I went down first, said good-bye to Frank's mom, and stepped outside. I stood in the sharp air, waiting, wondering what the holdup was when I heard a great muffled *boom*. Reflexively, I turned from the house. BBs, glass, and bits of wood rained against my hunting jacket. When I turned back, I saw a hole the size of a garbage can lid. The window mullions were gone, and the long reddish curtains hung from the blown-out frame like viscera. There was an unforgettable scream, the kind that stripped varnish from the soul, followed by a long silence. Then: "Oh God, oh Sweet Jesus!"

Mrs. Cone's terrified prayer was answered because, miraculously, nobody was injured, or almost. Frank's younger brother broke a filling when he got back to finishing his scrambled eggs, where a pellet had landed and hid itself.

Frank had loaded the shotgun in his room—a great taboo. Lee was only four feet from Frank. Had the barrel moved six or eight inches one way or another, Lee would have been cut in half. For once he was silent, his face sheet white. His hands could scarcely manage the small task of lighting a cigarette. He looked, I suppose, the way I had always wanted him to look: stripped of pretense and ugly with fear you could smell. His eyes jerked back and forth. He sobbed. His ears rang. He was going to be deaf, he whimpered. In the hallway, the acrid smell of cordite was overpowering.

MIKE YELLED AGAIN, "*Dad*, can I have a rifle?"

We walked past the livestock exhibit. I rolled the shell between my thumb and forefinger. The midway seethed with dust and a seedy vigor. An odor of pig dung rode the air.

Nero

Michael Malone

When you're on the road, there's nothing lonesomer than Christmas in New York City. Stores are lit up and couples are ice-skating under that big tree and sidewalks are full of strangers swinging red bags of presents and you start to thinking your life took a wrong turn on some old railroad line and is ending up in a field of frozen weeds. It's the sad sort of feeling makes me want to head home in a hurry. Or get married.

I was walking back to the hotel when I saw this man in a tuxedo crawling around in the display window of a bookstore, across a cloudy floor of fiberglass angels; the books stuck in their wire hands ran to corpses and blood. I stopped because there was a yellow cat in the window and that cat was so fat and imperious, it almost cheered me up.

I was still watching the cat when a tall woman jumped out of a taxi and hugged me. "My God, that you, Cuddy Mangum? You here for Will's party?"

"Darlin,' just ask me. Who's Will?"

It was Lauri Wald, NYPD. I'd met her last spring when we'd testified to Congress about how to stop Americans from shooting each other. "Don't let them buy guns," was my idea, but hey, who listens? Lauri and I'd gone out for meals and laughed and thought about taking things further, but somehow the moment had slipped away.

She had a forties look to her I loved, like she could march off with her red hair in a bandanna and her lunch in a metal box to weld a B-52 together. When I kissed her, I could smell the crisp winter night. "Lauri, you get that divorce?"

"I did." She looked me over. "Saw you in a magazine. 'Carolina Top Cop Stops Crime Cold.'"

My question made white puffs in the air. "You want to marry me?"

"Possibly."

Lauri's friend Will owned the store. She said he loved cops so much he'd be glad to have me come along to his Christmas party. As things turned out, that wasn't true.

The yellow cat led us up some spiral stairs into a paneled room with a tree decorated with guns and knives and skulls and such. Lauri introduced me to our host, the short man in the window. "Will Eberstark. Police Chief Cuddy Mangum from North Carolina."

"What's that, a state?" he asked me brusquely.

"State of mind."

He liked that. "You're tall."

"You got me there." I shook his hand.

"If you smoke, do it on the fire escape." The yellow cat was arching in and out of his feet like a tango dancer. "Scat!" He told us the cat was always climbing in through his bathroom window.

I said, "He looks like Nero Wolfe. Fat, wearing yellow pajamas."

Will liked that too. "He's my wife's cat. They live upstairs."

"Ex," Lauri said, and there was a whole story in that syllable.

He shoved Nero out of his way and went to greet the guests who kept flopping up the spiral stairs like salmon. The champagne was French, the caviar was Russian, and there was more of both than in *War and Peace*. Folks either drank nonstop or talked nonstop about how they'd given up drinking. Lauri pointed out two of her favorite crime writers. "Ted Keller, *Cutthroat*, and Brian Wells, *Mortal Lust*."

"I'm all for mortal lust," I told her.

We gave each other a smile that carries on a conversation by itself. It was interrupted by somebody's suddenly bellowing, "*She's* here!" We turned to look at a black-haired woman prowling through a cluster of blonds like a panther on the Discovery Channel, but a drunk one. Except for red earrings that blinked on and off, she was all in black—short black dress, long-legged black hose, and real high heels. "Who's that?" I asked Lauri.

Well, it was like saying, "Who's Michael Jordan?" to a Carolina basketball fan. "Tita Eberstark. You know, *To Love and to Perish*." According to Lauri, Will had never gotten over his best-selling wife, who'd divorced him but still lived on the fourth floor of his building, where—according to a gossip columnist—she had more dates than a platter of Moroccan couscous.

While the two writers hugged Tita, Will squeezed his champagne glass so hard he broke it. His ex just laughed, swooped up the cat, took off an earring, and hooked it through the collar. Nero couldn't shake it loose and ran around, blinking like a railroad crossing. Mrs. Eberstark floated her hand across Ted Keller's face. "Don't indulge Will," she purred. "He gobbles grief like a box of chocolates." She staggered into the crowd and the party swallowed her up.

Nero kept spinning like his tail was a string of firecrackers. Then, fat as he was, he leapt about a foot off the ground and threw himself at my knees. Finally I got that damn Christmas bell earring unhooked, and without a glimmer of gratitude, he thudded away. "You're welcome," I called.

The whole time, Will stood there sucking on his bloody hand. "I can't get over her," he told us all. "If she dropped dead, maybe. Please, kill her so I can get over her!"

"She's a bitch," *Cutthroat* reminded him. After Will left with the broken glass, he added, "We could kill her."

Mortal Lust shrugged. "Why not? We do it for a living."

I said, "I feel like you two oughta know, I'm a police chief." I nodded at Lauri. "And she's NYPD homicide."

The two writers must have thought I was joking, the way they laughed.

Another half hour and the party got so crowded Lauri and I had to hold our plates over our heads like Chinese acrobats. We were looking for Will to say good-bye when I felt Nero butting and biting at my calf. It was like he was trying to push me somewhere. He kept on meowing and shoving till we ended up at the bathroom. The air in there was sharp as a knife. I figured it was from the ice in the tub for the champagne, but Nero jumped up on the ledge and showed me that a big casement window was open.

"And your point, Fatso?" He ignored me, unless his tail twitch was a wisecrack. Then he pounced out the window onto the fire escape. I'd gotten so used to thinking of this cat as Nero Wolfe, it surprised me he'd go outside. He shouldn't have; he misjudged his jump and was hanging by his claws off that ladder like a clown in a yellow fat suit. I had to crawl out the window to grab him. That's when I saw Tita Eberstark, three stories below, lying dead in the passageway. Nobody alive could twist up her legs like that.

Lauri got the party quiet. When she made the announcement, I kept my eyes on *Cutthroat* and *Mortal Lust*. After all, I'd heard them discuss murdering the woman. But they looked run over by a truck; if it was an act, they ought to be playing the leads in their own TV series.

Soon as he heard his ex had fallen off the fire escape, Will went down like a plumb line, taking the Christmas tree with him. Guests ducked. He came to, moaning "Tita" like the saddest song you ever heard. His friends carried him over to a couch and consoled him about how they'd been expecting this sooner or later, the way she was drinking. He shouldn't' blame himself. Everybody knew he hadn't really wished her dead.

And maybe that would have been the end. Except for Nero the cat.

Could be Nero solved the case because I'd taken that damn blinking lightbulb off him, or maybe, who knows, he'd been hanging around all those books about smart detectives for so long, he thought he *was* Nero Wolfe. Or maybe he'd planted the evidence to avenge his dead owner, Mrs. Eberstark. Anyhow, he jumped up on the couch, walked down Will's torso to his ankles, and patted at his trouser leg. Will tried to kick him off, but he plopped right back.

Finally I noticed this weird pink luminescence glowing through one of Will's pant cuffs. I pulled out a little bell earring with a red blinking light. It was sticky. The other earring was still in my pocket.

Nero stared at me, the spooky way a cat will, like he was saying, "Use your head. You get it?" I gave it some thought. When I nodded, he twitched off.

Lauri didn't want to listen at first, but in the end she got it too.

Tita's bloody hair on a champagne bottle in the bathtub. Will's blood on the same bottle because he'd grabbed it with the hand he'd cut earlier. Her blood on the earring in his cuff. It took Lauri six hours to get Will to admit he'd smashed his ex on the head and shoved her off the fire escape. He claimed it was a jealous rage.

It was rage, OK, but more about the million dollars she had just demanded to move out of their building in midtown Manhattan; at the party *Cutthroat* had told her that Ukrainian developers wanted to buy it. She'd never gotten around to changing her will, and in her will Will got her half of the building. He'll have to sell it to pay his defense team.

Lauri took Nero home. She only had 700 square feet down near Union Square, but, hey, she couldn't just let him hang out on the fire escape.

Christmas Eve, on the way to the airport, all of a sudden I wondered "Why?" I told the cabdriver to swing around to Tiffany's, then I took that little blue bag and headed down to Union Square. It sounded like a good address.

There's nothing less lonesome in the world than waking up on Christmas Day in New York City with a woman in your arms and a fat yellow cat on your chest.

. . . .

In New York

Doug Marlette

Shortly after we arrived in the city of my dreams, Cameron and I attended our first New York dinner party. Gathered in the parlor of the sumptuous brownstone were a number of our neighbors—a world-famous heart surgeon, a legendary recluse novelist, a network anchorwoman and her investment banker husband, a pop music mogul and his wife, and a celebrated artist.

After some obligatory small talk, Rita, the hostess, introduced me to the artist, who was famous for his *Time* magazine cover portraits and sketches for the *New Yorker*. He was a short, balding man with small, raisinlike eyes and the face of a ferret, and I had admired his work immensely. "They tell me you're a famous political cartoonist," he said.

"Do they?"

"I never heard of you," he said.

Typical of New York, the men were all witty and acerbic and the women elegant and flirtatious, except for the woman who later glared at me across the dinner table like a prosecutor at the Nuremberg trial as I conversed with our hostess about the neighborhood preschool Wiley would be attending. My southern drawl seemed to unnerve her, to call to mind images of the gap-toothed banjo player from *Deliverance*. Every time I opened my mouth, my IQ dropped below room temperature. Finally, in a vaguely British accent she asked, "I gather you're not from around here?"

"No, ma'am," I said. "How could you tell?"

My attempt at levity seemed only to annoy her, and she quizzed me as though I were, indeed, a retarded child.

"Then where are you from exactly?"

"Charlotte, most recently," I said.

"Charlotte?" Her nose squinched, as if I had answered Kazakhstan.

"Yes, ma'am, but my people are from the North Carolina Piedmont. Alamance County, between Greensboro and Chapel Hill. Around Burlington, Graham, Saxapahaw, Mebane, Haw River, that area." I heard myself, like so many southerners with our overdeveloped sense of place, putting too fine a point on it, nailing down the locale with a kind of perverse specificity somehow motivated by an acute awareness of her infinite indifference.

"I don't see how anyone could possibly stand living down there with those people."

"Those people? You mean my kinfolks?"

"Surely your relatives are not . . ." She smirked at Rita. "Oh, you know . . ."

I felt my pulse quicken. "Actually, I don't."

"Well"—she quaffed her wine—"I'm certainly not going to explain."

"Have you ever been down South?" I asked.

"Once. I did a commercial shoot down there somewhere—"

"Felicity's a TV producer and filmmaker, Pick," Rita said, desperately trying to head off disaster. Cameron, sitting at the far end of the table, offered no help.

"Raleigh. That was it. Dreadful place. . . . I could never live down there."

Our hostess smiled diplomatically and asked, "Why not? I hear it's lovely."

Felicity looked at me. "I couldn't take all the racists down there."

"Yes," I said. "It's awful. So unlike this garden of racial harmony y'all got up here—Howard Beach, Bensonhurst, Crown Heights—hell, New York's a goddamn paradise of brotherly love!"

"How about some more roast duck?" Rita chirped, trying to pull the conversation out of the nosedive it had taken. She was right to be concerned. There was something about New Yorkers like my dinner companion that brought out every ounce of redneck defiance, awakened every strand of unreconstructed Confederate DNA, every rebellious "Fergit, Hell! Git Yore Heart in Dixie or Git Yore Ass Out!" impulse lying like a dormant virus in my bloodstream, and caused the years and decades to fall away and dropped me in a thicket dressed in a makeshift uniform of butternut and gray, squinting down the barrel of my squirrel gun at Chancellorsville.

"It's worse down there." Felicity was one of those spindly, fashion-conscious New York women, with an unerring instinct for self-caricature, whose choice of hairstyle and makeup only accentuated her most unflattering features. She had worked diligently to achieve a look that, as a man, I found grotesque and sexless but, as a cartoonist, I greatly appreciated. Her skin had the pallor of an anemic vampire, and her hair was tucked so tightly into her ballerina bun that it appeared to be painted on. Her earrings and jewelry were gigantic, possibly serving as ballast, counterweights to keep her facelifts tightly in place. Her dangling hoop earrings were so large I was tempted to set them on fire and wait for small animals to leap through them.

"Besides," she continued, "southerners just sound so . . . ignorant. I just can't take anything they say seriously. I'm a Democrat, of course, but I must say I could barely bring myself to vote for Jimmy Carter because of that accent of his."

"Well, ma'am"—the chill in my voice could have frozen hummingbirds in mid-flight—"where I come from we call that bigotry."

Devil's Island

Margaret Maron

"They say only madmen survive there." The captain spoke in a thick colonial patois. "These prisoners are more low than the lowest. Vile beasts. Men in name only. No decency, no—how you say?—*humanity*. How will such a one as you survive?"

The prisoner shrugged and looked down at his hands, uncallused nobleman's hands. "I learned woodworking as a child. Perhaps I'll take it up again." He tossed off the last of his wine, then leaned across the table to clasp the strong hand of the man who had become his friend during this long voyage to the most brutal penal colony in the Empire. "Don't worry, Captain. I'll survive. The emperor credits me with a traitorous ability to lead, to rally men to a cause. If he's right, I can help these wretched remnants of mankind—for they *will* be men, no matter how sunken in bestiality."

Before the captain could reply, a subordinate entered and saluted. "The patrol craft approaches, sir."

The captain stood heavily. "I must return to the bridge."

He wanted to offer the prisoner words of optimism, but when he looked at the finely bred boyish figure dressed in the absurd uniform of the colony—white robe, blue cloak, rough leather sandals—all optimism died.

There was a jarring metallic clang as the airlock of the patrol ship matched that of the starcruiser. The exchange was effected, then the patrol ship fell away, descending to the penal colony. In less than an hour, the captain received official notification: *"Prisoner released in that sector known to inmates as Judea."*

And all the way back to the civilized planets of the Empire, the captain wondered what form the prisoner's eventual madness would ultimately take.

viewmaster

Jill McCorkle

The ex-wife's picture hangs among others near the radiator in Roger's office. Theresa has trouble *not* looking at the photo even though she has studied and memorized every detail with a kind of tormenting curiosity. The other photos are linked to Roger's commercial real estate business—photo after photo of Roger shaking hands with local celebrities, the mayor; the anchor for the local news; Tripp Trout, owner of a seafood franchise who has never been seen without his fish mask. There are probably twenty such photos.

Beside the ex-wife is a younger, leaner Roger with dark hair and no lines around his eyes. He's smiling, and there is not a trace of worry or discontent; his hand cups the bare shoulder of the woman beside him: his wife, his mate. Her blond hair is shoulder length and feathered back from her face; her jeans are worn and flared, feet bare as she rests one leg over his. She leans in so their heads are touching. His other hand, wedding ring visible, is on her thigh as he hugs her close. He's wearing an old flannel shirt he still owns, one Theresa used to toss on in the middle of the night or after showering. She has not worn it since recognizing its connection to the past.

His daughter, just a toddler then, is in a little pink jacket off to the side. Her hair is yanked into high pigtails, something Theresa has heard Roger laugh and tease her about when they talk on the phone—*those tight pigtails did something to your brain, honey*, he always says. Now the daughter is in college on the west coast. Theresa has not met her though they have chatted on the phone in a friendly but awkward fashion until he is able to pick up—about Roger's work or the weather or Elsa, the old golden retriever who was just a puppy at the time of the divorce. The ex-wife, though several relationships and houses and career attempts beyond the marriage, continues to call and check in.

In the photo, they are a family of three on vacation in the mountains, dark shapes looming behind them in late afternoon light. There is a history behind them and several years still ahead. She looks once more at their entwined limbs, their child, the place Roger has said *they* should visit some time. It was where he had spent his childhood vacations. It was *his* place first. Theresa holds eye contact with the ex-wife and thinks: *I am here and you are way back there.*

But Roger is in both places.

"OH YOU WOULDN'T HAVE LIKED ME THEN," Roger said when he caught her studying the photo. She wanted to ask him why he kept it hanging, but before she could figure out how to ask, he was already telling the story of the day, his daughter covered in poison ivy by the end of it, the oatmeal bath and calamine lotion he bought and brought back to the motel room where his wife was studying for either the LSAT or to go to graduate school in library science—he couldn't remember which. She never pursued either one. What he could remember is that she didn't want him to watch the ball game on television or touch or talk to her. He described a perfectly awful time, and yet the photo remained like a door left wide open. Theresa wanted to ask, *Would you go back and fix it all if you could?*

Before Roger, most of her relationships were built on convenience, the result of sporadic and fleeting moments of boredom or lust. She had resisted an early conventional union that might— with good health and luck—have led to a golden wedding anniversary; and she had resisted repeating her own unhappy childhood by not having any children of her own. Instead, she had thrown all her time and energy into her work, assuring herself that someday she would find what was right for her, comforted by the idea of comfort.

"No one has everything," she was reminded countless times by friends who were getting married and having children. They were trying to emphasize her successful landscaping business, which is how she met Roger. She went from small window box and herb garden designs sold at the farmer's market to landscaping bank buildings and city plazas. Her brief engagement and a couple of meaningless relationships were all mixed up in her mind with abelia and dwarf gardenias and the Bradford pear trees all over town whose varying sizes documented her career.

WHEN SHE SEES Roger in the photograph, she feels oddly homesick. It's the same feeling she had as a kid staring into her Viewmaster at images of places so real she wanted to claim them as her own. As a ten-year-old her favorite reel was the one of Yellowstone National Park—hot springs and sunsets, red rock ledges so steep and close she was afraid to take a step while viewing. In the one of Old Faithful there was a man in plaid Bermuda shorts and a white dress shirt with his whole family in tow, which dated the photo and invaded her space. They did not belong in her life. She loved the moose in the snow, the almost navy sky, but most of all she loved the black bears, so real she wanted to reach out and stroke their fur, shocked when she did and touched nothing but air.

THERE IS ANOTHER PHOTO of a much younger Roger in front of the old E&R Drive-in before it was torn down and replaced by a Food Lion. It was a fixture in the area, catering to the Saturday night dates of a three-county region. Roger was one of the many supporters who tried to save it. And so was she. Somewhere in the huge gathering of people spilling beyond the frame, she knows she is there. So is Tripp Trout, Roger has said, but very few people know what he looked like before the mask.

"So we could have met twenty years ago," he said. "Been together so long we'd be sick of each other or maybe in counseling by now."

"You were already married."

"And you were engaged."

"You said I wouldn't have liked you back then."

"But I lied. What were you wearing?"

"Levis, T-shirt, Birkenstocks," she said. "I was real original."

"Wait. I *do* remember you," he said. "I tried to pick you up but you ignored me."

"No, I tried to pick *you* up but you said you had to ask your wife."

NOW THEY REFER often to *the day we never met* and have pinpointed other possible intersections, the ghosts of their younger selves acting out all the parts they never got to play. In fact, she once drove by that very place in the mountains where he used to go. She might have stopped for gas and walked into the very store he went in to buy that oatmeal bath. She could have met him then. She could have said, "Bad day, huh?"

"How much time do you have and I'll tell you."

"I have more time than I know what to do with."

SHE TURNS OFF THE LIGHT in his office and makes her way to the darkened bedroom where Roger is stretched out sleeping, Elsa snoring at his feet. She reaches out to familiar shapes, window, wall, brittle unnourished ficus she is attempting to resurrect, chair with his jeans slung over the back, table the ex-wife never would have lived with. She finds the footboard, Elsa's blanket. Fur, flannel, skin. Under the weight of her hand, his chest moves up and down.

. . . .

Birds Are Entangled by Your Feet and Men by Their Tongue

Philip McFee

That's what his fortune says, so, taken aback, he decides to open his friend's cookie as well. *You have a quiet and unobtrusive nature.* There's been a mistake. This has to be his and the cryptic pronouncement must have been meant for someone else. After lunch, at work, over dinner, he can't get it out of his mind. That night he has a dream.

He's a member of the Swiss Family Robinson, and everyone is racing around their bamboo, tree-slung mansion on ostriches. As he draws into the lead, his massive bird kicking up dust as it blows through luscious thickets and tropical glades, his foot jams in the ostrich's legs like a broomstick in bike spokes. They both crash to the ground. Bloodied, possibly blind in one eye, he rises and tries to sprint away. He can do this. He can finish the race alone.

But before he can leave, a moist, sandpaper rope wraps around his ankle and he tumbles to the ground. Like a frog, his ostrich, still lolling on its side, has ensnared him with its enormous, grainy tongue. Surely it will devour him. There's been a mistake. He has a quiet and unobtrusive nature. He will taste terrible.

sheridan Drive-in

John McNally

The Sheridan, at the corner of 79th and Harlem, was our nearest drive-in movie theater. It was a dusty parking lot with a few hundred lead posts poking up out of the gravel. Each post held a cast-iron speaker. At the center of the lot was a low-to-the-ground concrete bunker where concessions were sold and where the projectionist ran the movie. When my parents took me and my sister, Kelly, to the Sheridan, we sometimes had to drive around to find a speaker that worked. My father, cursing each time one wouldn't click on, would eventually say, "I'll try one more, and if *that* one doesn't work, I'm getting a refund." But the last one always worked, maybe because the odds were leaning in our favor with each bad speaker, or maybe because we'd end up parking several rows behind everyone else and the speakers back there hadn't been used much.

When we first started going to the Sheridan, my parents owned a Rambler. My father didn't like to run the heat during the movie— "We'll burn up all our gas," he'd say—so on cold nights we'd bring blankets and pile them up on top of us. Kelly would kick me under the blankets and then blame me for starting it.

"*Both* of you better cut it out," my father'd say, "or this is the last thing we'll ever do together as a family, you hear me?"

The truth is, it was the *only* thing we ever did together besides live in the same house, but the threat always hinted to other, more interesting things, all of which would vanish if we didn't cut it out. I wanted to ask if there were things that I was forgetting, but I knew that this question would set my father off. I was always setting one or the other of my parents off with questions I'd ask before I really thought them through.

During our dozen years of going to the Sheridan, we saw probably fifty or sixty movies, but the ones I remembered best were *Easy Rider*, *Planet of the Apes*, *The Chinese Connection*, *Beneath the Planet of the Apes*, *Buster and Billie*, *Escape from the Planet of the Apes*, *Walking Tall*, *Conquest of the Planet of the Apes*, *Enter the Dragon*, and *Battle for the Planet of the Apes*. The few times I made the mistake of going with someone else's parents, I saw *The Love Bug* and a movie called *Gus* about a mule that played football.

Every night was a double feature. The first movie was always the one that everyone in the world wanted to see, but I liked going to the Sheridan for other reasons. For starters, I liked intermission. A black-and-white movie of a clown pointing to a ticking clock played on the screen to show how much time you had left to buy hot dogs. On those rare occasions when my father would give me money to get everyone a hot dog, I would walk by the projectionist's booth and look at the man inside. It was the same man each time, an old guy with a pencil-thin mustache, the kind of mustache Bud Abbott had, and he would always be smoking a cigarette and reading a magazine. One time I walked in front of the concession stand and jumped up with my arm in the air, and the shadow of my hand appeared on the screen, magnified to at least twelve feet high and three feet wide. When I got back to the car, I wanted to ask if anyone had seen my incredibly big hand, but my father was complaining about how little ice was in the cooler, and how his beer, sitting on top of everyone else's drinks, was now too warm to enjoy. Kelly, sound asleep or pretending to be sound asleep, was nothing more than a lump under the covers. I handed over to my mother the hot dogs, each one slipped into a shiny aluminum bag so that they looked like miniature rocket ships.

"If Kelly doesn't wake up," Dad said, "I'll take her hot dog. She'll never know, right?"

The other thing that I liked about going to the Sheridan was the second movie because there were always a lot of naked women in them. My parents liked to believe that I had fallen asleep by the time the movie had gotten to the racy parts, and I'd even go so far as to shut my eyes.

111

"Are they asleep?" my father always asked at the appearance of the first naked woman.

My mother'd turn around and say, "Kelly's asleep. I can't tell about Hank. He's still sitting up." And then she'd call out to me in a heavy whisper: "*Hank. Are you asleep? Hank. You're not watching this, are you?*"

As soon as she turned back around, I'd open my eyes just a little so that they were narrow slits through which I could watch the movie. Usually, the movies were about women who'd gone bad, women who were in prison at the very beginning of the movie, or women who weren't bad to begin with but who ended up bad in prison anyway. I imagined girls from my school—Mary Polaski or Peggy Petropulos—handcuffed and put together in a dark jail cell. I imagined myself as a prison guard, smacking my billy club against my palm, walking back and forth in front of their cell, waiting for one or the other of them to pee. Peeing always played a big role in these movies.

No matter how hard I tried not to, I would fall asleep at some point during the movie, dreaming of girls from my class, all of them now in prison, and when I woke up, I was either slung over my father's shoulder or I was already in my own bed, my body curled like a fist. Only once did I wake up during the movie itself, and my mom and dad were in the front seat kissing. I'd never seen them kiss like this, on the mouth, the way men and women kiss in movies. On the screen behind them was a woman who, having escaped from prison, was being chased by a pack of vicious dogs. I couldn't actually see the face of the woman being chased because we were seeing everything through her eyes. The dogs were barking behind us, getting louder, catching up to us, while jagged tree branches scratched our arms and fallen tree trunks caused us to trip and stumble. My mother said to my father, "OK, that's enough," and my father leaned back away from her. Without a word, he rolled down the window and returned the speaker to its hook. Then he started the car and backed out of our space.

Was this what they did each time we went to the movies? Did they kiss until my mother said they'd had enough?

As Dad circled the parking lot, I could still hear the tinny barks and growls of angry dogs. I had to swivel in my seat to keep watching the movie, but as my father pulled out of the Sheridan and turned onto Harlem Avenue, the screen got smaller and smaller, until finally it all disappeared, leaving the four of us alone—me, my sister the lump, my mother picking up trash and stuffing it into a too-small bag, and my father behind the wheel. My father's eyes kept darting up to the rearview mirror, and I imagined that the pack of dogs, having jumped from the screen, was following us, gaining on us, and that my father was doing what needed to be done to save us, but you could tell by the haunted look in his eyes that he feared he would fail.

The Escapee

Heather Ross Miller

My sister Jo disappeared on New Year's Day in the mountains of North Carolina where she went skiing with Steve, the guy she's been dating. I'm going to go look for her. I'm fourteen. Mama says I'd never survive. But I've learned things about survival.

Jo's up there where that escapee Eric Rudolph is. He blew up abortion clinics with bombs. He killed and maimed people. I saw the nurse on TV with a thousand nail holes in her. I dreamed that night it was Jo, those nail holes red as measles, and I cried in my sleep.

It gets colder in the mountains. I hope Jo has a parka. I bet Eric Rudolph has a parka and some blankets. I hope he gives her one.

Mama said Jo ran off to marry Steve because she was pregnant. I think that's OK because once Jo tells Eric she's pregnant, he won't shoot her. This is after he shoots Steve. I don't like Steve. I don't see how my sister let him get her pregnant.

That escapee could have got Jo pregnant, I bet, just looking at her. He looks like Jesse James in the papers. You'd never think you were looking at a crazed born-again killer. I see them around a campfire, snow falling in the dark pines. Steve lies far off behind a log and snow covers him. Jo forgets him because Eric Rudolph talks to her and tells her things she likes. How they will live in the mountains and steal stuff from people's vacation houses, rich people who won't miss a can of peaches in heavy syrup, a block of cheddar. Steve would never think of such smart things.

I want to find Jo and tell her this is OK. That escapee will not shoot her. And even when the FBI comes to get Eric Rudolph, they won't get her or the baby. Jo and the baby will slip on back into the

114

woods and live in caves and eat cans of peaches in heavy syrup and blocks of cheddar from the rich people.

I am making plans to leave Mama and disappear too, just like Jo and Eric Rudolph. I know he will have to go to jail soon because he did mean things and he can't get out of paying for it. But Jo and the baby and I will not. While Steve rots in briars and vines, we will harvest the wilderness and never think about him. Or Mama. Every night around the campfire, Jo and I will cuddle her baby and sing and think about the escapee and how he taught us to do this.

walking Bird

Lydia Millet

One of the birds was lame, struggling gamely along the perimeter of the fence. The bird was large, a soft color of blue, and rotund like a pheasant or a hen. Its head was adorned with a crown of hazy blue feathers, which had the curious effect of making it seem at once beautiful and stupid.

A family watched the bird. It was a small family: a mother, a father, and a little girl.

The fat blue bird had white tape on one knee and lurched sideways when it stepped down on the hurt limb. The little girl sat on the end of a wooden bench to watch the bird, and the mother and father, tired of walking and glad of the chance for a rest, sat down too.

This was inside the zoo's aviary, an oval garden with high fences and a ceiling of net. Here birds and visitors were allowed to commingle. Black-and-white stilts stood on straw-thin legs in a shallow cement pond, and bleeding heart doves strutted across the pebbly path, looking shot in the chest with their flowers of red.

The little girl watched the lame bird solemnly as it hobbled around the inside of the fence. There was something doggedly persistent in the bird's steady and lopsided gait; it did not stop after one rotation, nor after two. The little girl continued to gaze. At first the mother and the father watched the little girl as she watched the bird, smiling tenderly; then the mother remembered a household problem and asked the father about it. The two began to converse.

The zoo was soon due to close for the day, and the aviary was empty except for the family and the birds. Small birds hopped among the branches and squawked. Large birds stayed on the ground and sometimes made a quick dash in one direction, then turned suddenly and dashed back.

A keeper came into the aviary in a grubby baseball cap and clumpy boots. The little girl asked her why the lame bird did not fly instead of walking. The keeper smiled and said it was a kind of bird that walked more than it flew.

"But can it fly?" asked the little girl. "Could it fly if it wanted to fly?"

The keeper said it probably could, and then she moved off and did something with a hose. The mother and father talked about flooring.

The little girl got off the bench and followed the lame bird, clucking and bending and trying to attract its attention. It ignored her and continued to walk along the inside of the fence, around and around and around.

The aviary was not large, so each circuit was completed quickly. But the bird did not stop and the girl did not stop. After a while the father remembered his life outside the aviary, his office and car and his stacks of paper. His presence in the aviary became instantly ridiculous to him. He got up from the bench and told the little girl it was time to go. The little girl said no, she was not ready. She wanted to stay with the bird. The father said that was too bad. The little girl tried to bargain. The father became angry and grabbed the little girl's arm. The little girl began to cry, and the mother waved the father away.

It was several minutes before the mother could fully comfort the little girl. During this time the father left the aviary and opened his telephone. He paced and talked into the telephone while the mother sat on the bench with the little girl, an arm around her shoulders. He waved to the mother and pointed: he would wait for them in the car.

The mother told the little girl her father loved her very much, only he was busy. He had stress and pressure. He did not mean to frighten her by grabbing. The little girl nodded and sniffed.

When the little girl was no longer agitated, her mother wiped the tears from her face and the little girl looked around. She told her mother she could not see her bird anymore. Her mother put away her tissue and then looked around too. The bird was not visible. Through the leaves in the trees came a glancing of light; the stainless steel dishes were empty of birds. The water in them was still.

The mother looked for large birds on the dirt of the ground and did not see them. She stood and looked for small birds in the green of branches but did not see them either.

"Where is my bird?" asked the little girl.

The mother did not know. She did not see the lame bird, and she did not see the other birds. She did not even hear them.

And yet time had barely passed since the birds were all there. The mother had barely looked away from the birds, she thought now. She had only attended for a few minutes to her child's brief and normal misery.

"It's time to go, anyway," said the mother, and she looked at her watch. "The zoo is closing."

The little girl said that maybe the birds flew out at night, through the holes in the net into the rest of the world.

The mother said maybe. Maybe so.

As they left the aviary, the little girl was already forgetting the bird. She would never think of the bird again.

There was almost no one left in the zoo, none of the day's visitors. But it seemed to the mother that the visitors she did see, making their way to the turnstiles, were all walking with a slight limp, an unevenness. She wondered if they could all be injured, every single one of them debilitated; but surely this was impossible. Unless, the mother thought, the healthy ones had left long ago, and what she now saw were the stragglers who could not help but be slow.

Ahead of her the limping people went out and vanished.

Along the path to the exit, the cages seemed empty to the mother: even the reeds around the duck ponds faded, and the signs with words on them and images of flamingos. The mother looked upward, blinking. In the sky there was nothing but airplanes and the bright sun.

The mother's eyes felt dazzled. The sky and the world were all gleaming a terrible silver. How she loved her daughter. Urgently she took hold of the little girl's hand. She felt a brace of tears close her throat.

Why? It had been a fine day.

The Music Lover

Katherine Min

Gordon Spires lived across the courtyard from Leonard Hillman, concert master of the M—— Symphony, and his lover, Kyoung Wha Jun, the second violinist. Leonard and Kyoung Wha often practiced together outside in the courtyard, under the brim of a large oak tree. The neighbors would hear them playing Debussy or Brahms and sometimes something contemporary that they wouldn't recognize.

Gordon liked to listen to them. He was in love with Kyoung Wha, who was slender and lovely, and he believed that she secretly returned his affection but could only reveal it through her music. So when she played Mozart, it was because he was Gordon's favorite, and when she played Bach, it meant that she was biding her time, and when she played Tchaikovsky, it was surely a sign that she was ready to run off. For it was well known that Leonard beat Kyoung Wha when he was drunk, that he cheated on her with the first violist, and that he had not quit smoking like he told Kyoung Wha he would but snuck cigarettes after matinee performances. At least these things were well known to Gordon, who was sickly and often home during the day.

One Sunday afternoon in late autumn, Kyoung Wha and Leonard played Beethoven. From his bedroom window, Gordon could see them, Kyoung Wha in a pleated blue skirt with prim white blouse, her long bangs swinging in her face as she swept her bow across the strings of her violin; Leonard, his narrow face impassive, eyes closed, chin tilted up at an unpleasant angle. Gordon could distinguish the rich, vibrant tones of Kyoung Wha's playing from the darker, ruminative vibrations of Leonard's, and he attributed the mistakes—rushed tempo, inconsistent meter, mawkish drawing out of notes—to Leonard, who was, in Gordon's opinion, the inferior of the two musicians.

Taking careful aim, Gordon threw a Monopoly piece—a silver top hat—at the rounded, balding place at the back of Leonard's head. Leonard did not stop. Gordon threw the wheelbarrow, the thimble, and the Scottish terrier. He used more force.

"What the—?"

Beethoven came to a halt. Gordon peeked to see Leonard rubbing his bald patch, looking up at the oak tree, then down to the ground. Leonard shrugged at Kyoung Wha, who shrugged back. They resumed playing.

The next day, Gordon lobbed a satsuma, just grazing Leonard's left temple. Leonard leapt from his chair. Kyoung Wha seemed to look straight at Gordon then, smiling sadly. Even crouched below his bedroom window, he could feel her smile penetrate his heart like the most tender of arrows.

A few days passed before they played outside again, Leonard setting up in what had formerly been Kyoung Wha's spot, farthest from Gordon's window, Kyoung Wha moving farther from Leonard, into a sunny patch that did not get much shade. Her face in sunlight looked faded to Gordon, wan, and when she played—Mendelssohn this time—he heard the silent suffering as separate notes from the ones that overlapped with Leonard's, inhabiting the spaces between. She was even more beautiful in her despair, black hair against pale complexion, in an autumnal ensemble of mauves and rusts.

Gordon heaved a bottle of multivitamins, but it overshot its mark, landing, with a muffled plop, in a giant hosta.

It rained for several days after that, the afternoons overhung with mist. Gordon saw Kyoung Wha come into the courtyard in a yellow rain slicker. He thought her green rain boots splendid, as were the orange bill and bubble eyes on her hood, which were meant to make her look like a duck.

On the first clear day, Leonard appeared without Kyoung Wha. He began to play Mahler, his feet planted like andirons before a hearth. Gordon disliked the implication that music could simply go on without her. He wondered where she was, what Leonard had done to her. The lights were off in their apartment. He could see the white fringe of an afghan against the window, resting on the back of a blood red sofa.

Gordon palmed a large rock shaped like a dinosaur egg, with a rough, pock-marked surface. He raised the window and hurled it. The rock rainbowed up and out, hitting Leonard squarely on top of the head and bouncing off. The strings of the violin made a distressed, bleating sound as Leonard slumped sideways out of his chair, then fell face first against the brick walkway.

Time passed. The lights went on. Gordon saw Kyoung Wha come out, heard her call Leonard's name. Approaching his body, she kneeled, bent to retrieve his violin by its broken neck, got up, and stumbled back inside. The lights went out.

Gordon listened, but all he heard was the sound of distant traffic.

Softly, he closed the window.

HOW to ROll

Courtney Jones Mitchell

In a secluded park on the good side of town, while the crickets talk among themselves and the nosy stars spy through the trees at their naked bodies, Stan tells Barbara he is moving far away. He is involved in International Relations. Barbara has never been quite clear on the specifics, but she has seen Stan wake in the mornings and dress in sleek black suits to go his office downtown where he internationally relates.

"I don't think that you should wait for me, Barbie," he says.

He cups Barbara's shoulder with his hand and gives it a little shake as if she'd just been defeated in a Little League game. Barbara imagines him with baseball gloves and cleats. *Good game.*

For the breakup, Stan has chosen a park in a classic-looking neighborhood near his college town where his classic-looking mother grew up. She receives *Vanity Fair* by mail, and Stan has mentioned this more than once. Stan looks around the park appreciatively as if someone has laid it out especially for him. He approves of the work. He eyes the old wooden gazebo, the picnic tables, and the lush growth of late summer. "You know, I really love this town. This town has history."

They sit up and Stan drapes his sweating arm around her. Will she be replaced by a more exotic woman overseas? Barbara has never been overseas and she is less than exotic. She wears white Keds tennis shoes, and on nights when she is not with Stan, she wears pants held up by an elastic waistband.

There are no words for being dumped while you're naked. Where are the pockets for shoving your hands down deep while you stare at the ground? Where is the skirt hem to unravel while you pretend to listen? Where do you wipe your tears?

Stan concentrates on buttons and zippers. "Then we're good here?"

Barbara is almost sure he winks, but who can tell in this dark? She leans her head back, her hair grazing the grass. She sees the world upside down. The kudzu-covered trees look like friendly, furry monsters.

"See, Barbie, look here. You can see my grandparents' house!" Stan points to a light squeezing between two elms. Barbara hates that nickname. Barbie is a plastic doll who, even with her limited range of motion, is more accomplished than Barbara, who teaches classes at You Look Marvelous!, a diet center for women. Barbara follows his finger to the light. His grandfather, whose family emigrated from Greece, is the youngest of nine children. He attended college on a scholarship and is a self-made man.

"He is probably listening to a baseball game on his radio tonight." Barbara removes dirt from her fingernails. She didn't really know her grandfather. He was a drunk.

"Cheer up!" Stan says and pinches Barbara's leg. When Barbara flinches, he looks disappointed.

"Oh, Barbie, you understand. You must."

How can Barbara explain how she feels, or this hot, sad thing inside her? She's entered a tunnel, vacuum cleaner bag, or one of those machines that seals your food in plastic. How could she have been so wrong?

Maybe all along Stan was a snake, but it's hard to admit such a dirty thing in such a pretty neighborhood. She'd thought that one day she'd marry Stan and move into his classically columned house on Water Street. After months and months of dating, they had never discussed marriage, but Barbara kept fantasies and a copy of *Southern Bride* tucked under the mattress like a pornographic magazine. Time was running away, and she'd been dreaming her whole life of chasing it down the aisle.

"Besides," he says, clearing his throat and tugging at the collar of his oxford, "I'm not sure I would wait for you. We're humans, right? Adults. And I've got wanderlust. It's in my blood, my *heritage* to want to see the world." He nods toward his grandfather's house. He places his hand over hers, dwarfing it.

Stan has made a statement of fact, as if facts could explain the dark turning of the heart, the way it can ossify or grow black. He plucks a blade of grass as they walk to his car. Barbara has no breath and her insides are blistering. She crosses her hands over her chest like little girls receiving their First Communions or the suspected witches pressed to death by layers of stones.

IN THE CAR she stays close to the door, keeping her fingers on the handle so she can jump out if she needs to. She's seen this on television shows; Barbara knows how to roll. She is suddenly certain she could lift the car, if need be. She could even eat it, she could rip through the steel like a steak. She could shatter the windows with a bare hand, jump out to the sidewalk, and sprint until the soles of her Keds split.

Barbara could do lots of things—deliver twin babies in a falling elevator, perform tracheotomies using only a wooden spatula and the back of her earring, win a Showcase Showdown on *The Price Is Right*. She would shine on television, turn some heads.

Her fists curl and her heartbeats make dents in her chest. When she whips up the emergency brake, they both fly. As they crash through the windshield, her hands passing delicate snowflakes of glass and her backside meeting the cool slick of the hood with a thump, every particle on her skin is welcome, unexpected. Her fall is perfectly choreographed, a stunt-double somersault. She turns, as if being photographed by her paparazzi, just in time to see Stan's confused, plastic face good-byeing and good-lucking in the opposite direction until the air swallows him and he can be heard no more.

Ten words or More

Ruth Moose

The woman on the phone is from the insurance company checking to see if I'm eligible for premium long-term care insurance, if I still have any of my marbles. I'm a new widow and have a cheaper LTC policy with the same company. I'm in a hurry, and tell her, but she wants to give me a list of ten words I'm to use in a sentence and repeat back to her.

"Packet," she says in my ear.

I wait, jiggling my foot.

"Packet," she repeats.

I wait for the other nine words, look at my watch.

"Packet," she repeats louder and with a sharpish edge to her voice.

"And . . . . ." I say. "What's the next word?" Really in a hurry. How long can ten words take? "And what?"

"You tell me," she says, "in a sentence."

"Oh," I say. "Is this like a packet of paper? A packet of sugar? What?"

"Packet," she says again, really impatient now. "Like you have on your clothes."

"Oh, pocket? Pock-it," I say. "You aren't from the South, are you? Where are you?"

"Ohio," she snaps.

"I have two pockets on my jeans," I say.

"Grass," she says.

"The kind you mow or the kind you smoke?"

"Either," she snaps again.

She's asked earlier if I lived alone. This was after she'd run through the facts of my age, marital status, and so forth. I had been halfway out the door to teach my Monday class and running late.

"I don't have any grass," I said. "Of either kind." The Ohio voice has no sense of humor. I expected a little chuckle at least.

"Key," she asks.

"I lost my office key," I answer.

"Mirror." She's moving right along.

"I avoid mirrors." Silence.

"Razor?" She's all business.

"When my husband died I brought his razor home. I still have it."

"Fountain?"

"The garden outside the hospital had a fountain." Now I'm crying, crying, sobbing, choking sobs.

"Repeat as many of the words as you can remember," Miss All Business Voice says. "Starting now."

I can't stop crying. I hang up the phone. I have probably failed the test.

The Pounding

Robert Morgan

Jevvie had been warned that neighbors and church members might drop by on Saturday night. Effie Croft had stopped by to ask how Alvin was and told her they might have visitors on Saturday, if that was OK. Jevvie said of course it was. But the truth was it made her nervous to think of people crowding into their living room. One of the deacons or the preacher was sure to lead in prayer. Though she went to church herself when she could, religion outside the church embarrassed Jevvie. And she was always ashamed of Alvin's drinking, his arrests and stays in the hospital.

The week before when they brought Alvin home from the VA hospital in Asheville, dried out and pale, he'd promised not to ever drink liquor again. "I'll believe that when I see it," Jevvie had told him.

"Believe what you want, old woman," Alvin said. His logging truck sat in the backyard gathering rust. His chainsaw lay on the porch leaking a shadow of oil. She'd moved the bed into the living room by the stove so he would be warm while he regained his strength.

The Masons arrived first on Saturday evening, and when she saw Laurie Mason place a brown paper bag on the table, she thanked her. "It's just some dark-roast coffee," Laurie said. But when Johnny Herman arrived with a box of Vienna sausages, Jevvie knew it was a pounding. She was more embarrassed than ever, for only when somebody was out of money and out of luck did the neighbors gather, each bringing a pound of something, a pound of dried beans, a pound of lard, Spam. Jevvie felt her face get hot. "You shouldn't have," she said to Linda Miller.

"What are neighbors for?" Preacher Wilson blustered and placed a bag on the table.

Jevvie greeted each couple as they came through the door. Some carried gifts wrapped like Christmas presents. Alvin lay propped up on the bed, nodding to those who gathered by the stove. They were curious to see how he looked after the DWI arrest, after the DTS.

"We just wanted to drop by and wish you well," Preacher Wilson said. He led in a short prayer, asking a blessing on Sister Jevvie and Brother Alvin, and then the group sang "We Gather Together to Ask the Lord's Blessing." All the time Jevvie was thinking she didn't have a thing to serve them, no cider or lemonade. When the singing stopped she said, "I'll make some coffee."

"No need to do that, Sister Jevvie," Preacher Wilson said. "We just came by to fellowship for a little while."

"Why don't you open the packages," Bessie Hudson said, as if it was a shower instead of a pounding. The table was piled with bags and boxes and wrapped gifts. Jevvie stepped to the table and opened the first bag and pulled out a canned ham. The second bag held a jar of olives. Each time she opened a package she said thank you, and the people clapped. There was a pound of bacon in one box, a toaster in another. There was jam and honey. "I don't know how to thank you all," she said.

She opened each present and held it up for all to see. Alvin thanked the guests also, his voice low and shaking. When Jevvie reached for the final bag, her hands began to tremble as she lifted out a quart bottle of Four Roses whiskey. The room got so quiet you could hear the flames whisper in the stove. "Thank you all so much," Jevvie said.

Tumbleweed

Shelia Moses

My man is like a tumbleweed. He just rolls around and catches everything that crosses his path—every woman that is. I am telling you he's just like a tumbleweed. That is the reason I did not want to come to this one-horse town to live. But Hogwood, North Carolina, is my Tumbleweed's home, and he wanted to come back to be near his dying daddy. That was four years ago. His daddy, Mr. Pop, is still alive. So why are we still here?

I knew Tumbleweed would start rolling with the gals that used to love him as soon as the train stopped in Weldon to let us off in 1952. We was only here one day before we ran into one of his old gals, Missy, in the grocery store. That was the beginning of Tumbleweed going back to his old ways. First he told me that Missy was his cousin. Then I looked at that boy of hers, Boone, and I knew Tumbleweed was lying. I knew he was the daddy. Look more like Tumbleweed than Tumbleweed look like himself.

"Come on Sweet Ida," he said to me.

"Come on nothing, Tumbleweed. You lied to me again. You know good and well Missy ain't your cousin. You know that boy is your boy."

"Na'll Ida, Boonie ain't no boy of mine. I only got six boys and two girls. You know that." He say that mess like he proud that he left a baby in every town between Wildwood, New Jersey, and Hogwood. He ain't never had no wife, so what he bragging for?

Missy ain't saying a word. She just smiling and turning from side to side like she can't stand still around my Tumbleweed. That boy Boonie ain't got good sense. He don't even know what we talking about. Guess we better leave before he eat up all the candy in the grocery store that Missy ain't even offered to pay for. He definitely Tumbleweed's boy because he always want *something for nothing*. Can't be too crazy, now can he?

"Oh stop looking for reasons not to love me gal." Then Tumbleweed pulled me in his arms in the store that was filled with people. The store always filled with people from Rich Square, Jackson, and Hogwood on a Friday evening. It's payday, even for the field hands. The womenfolks was looking when Tumbleweed pulled me closer. I forgot all about that boy that looked just like my man. I remembered all the reasons I love myself some Tumbleweed.

I love him for the same reason all these North Carolina womenfolks love him.

He a man! A real man! My man!

He ain't all fine or nothing. He just a man that you gots to have.

Come that Monday morning we was back working in the 'bacco field. I was hanging 'bacco in the hot barn loft while Tumbleweed drove the truck for Mr. Willie who own all this land and 'bacco. Right now he ain't driving. Tumbleweed just sitting and waiting to take us home. I think Mr. Willie had extra folks in the field that day. Extra women to prime this 'bacco. Extra women to look at my Tumbleweed.

They can't fool me. That old Bessie was there shaking her big behind all over the place. She the only woman I know that wear tight skirts in the 'bacco barn. I can't believe I left my job waiting tables at that rich country club in Wildwood to come here to prime 'bacco. Tumbleweed claimed it is a good way to make a living.

Look at him sitting over there looking at me up here in the loft and all the other women that love him out in the field.

"You want some water?" Bessie yelled to my Tumbleweed when it was time for us to knock off for lunch.

He did not answer her.

He better not!

"Anything Tumbleweed want, I can get for him," I said, climbing down the hot barn loft for lunch.

"Fine," Bessie said as she laughed like she knew something that I did not know. "I can get Tumbleweed some water later tonight," she whispered and walked over to the tree to eat her pork and beans and crackers.

"Say it again," I said as I ran up behind her. Bessie turned around in slow motion. She must have eyes in the back of her head.

I did not get far when them sisters of hers all jumped up from the ground at the same time.

"Where you going city girl?" her oldest sister Pennie Ann asked as she rolled up the sleeves on her shirt while kicking her can of beans out of the way.

I will fight anybody, anywhere for my Tumbleweed, I thought to myself.

I tried to roll up my sleeves too.

That is all I remember. The next thing I know I am lying in the back of Tumbleweed's truck and he's looking down at me.

"How many fights you going to have girl?" he said like he was almost sad.

"How many women you gonna love Tumbleweed?" I said as I reached for my head that was really hurting now. The knot on it felt mighty big.

Tumbleweed leaned over me and kissed me real hard with his big black lips.

All the women folks looked at us. They wished they was me.

Revolutionaries

Lawrence Naumoff

Jeffrey and Anna move from Carrboro to Chatham County and rent a house between Chicken Bridge and Bynum, overlooking the Haw River. The house has no running water, no bathroom, not even a sink. Living like that is so very cool in the 1970s because even though they've grown up rich and privileged, once they are at UNC, they imagine themselves radical artists and so very not middle class, like their dull and narrow-minded families back in Winston-Salem and Charlotte. They read 1930s populist literature and discover the "noble working class," who are still tragically exploited. "Exploited" becomes one of their favorite words.

They meet a man named Taffy who owns a service station/grocery store in Bynum and who has a rebel flag on the wall behind the counter, one on the front of his truck, one on his cap, and one on his belt opposite the letters CSA. His wife, who looks like the other woman from *Bonnie and Clyde*, not Faye Dunaway but the beleaguered one, keeps the store clean, the bathrooms clean, and serves him lunch everyday, rushing home to have it ready by 12 noon on the dot.

Jeffrey and Anna are there one time when she is late, and Taffy yells at her and ignores the food and gets a small Coke and a Snickers bar and eats that while she packs back up and leaves. Jeffrey and Anna feel embarrassed, but there must be a reason. Maybe Taffy's spirit has been broken by working for The Man, or the oil companies, for too long, because otherwise he does seem kind of noble and they try to understand him.

They farm a little and listen to old records, start a garden, and throw away the new television set her parents have given them, leaving it on top of the dumpster for some poor family to have. He has long hair and it is as blond and as beautiful as Anna's, who begins to wear hers in a long braid, so that she looks like a Swedish Indian. Once they show up at Mt. Something Church, they aren't sure of the name, on a Sunday morning, it seems the right thing to do, to fit in, and they park their Volvo wagon (they forget to take the antiwar bumper stickers off!) in the midst of all the Buicks and Silverados, but the minister talks about patriotism and moral turpitude, so they give up on the church idea and smoke just the right amount of dope that afternoon and fall asleep on the porch, side by side, with their cat and dog nearby.

One evening they take a walk through the Bynum mill village and come upon a wood-carving primitive artist and try to buy something from him, but he won't take any money, he just outright gives them two fantasy animal sculptures. They've never met anyone this pure before, and they cry on the way home.

Late that night they return and leave ten $20 bills in an envelope in his mailbox. They go back to their old shack and make beautiful love all night long, in the field and down at the pond, they just feel like they are a part of something so beautiful they have to express it as deeply as they can.

As time goes on, they begin to go to Taffy's store for lunch, even though no one talks to them and the men hanging around get real quiet, but they understand this because the men have been exploited so long they don't trust anyone. Jeffrey and Anna buy Vienna sausages and hoop cheese (so greasy it tastes like orange lard) and usually stand around for a few minutes waiting for Taffy's wife to show up so they can smile at her and be helpful if possible.

Soon, they have an idea. They decide to make a surprise lunch not only for Taffy and his wife but enough for anyone who might be in the store at that time, putting on a kind of impromptu Workers' Picnic. They buy a cured ham from a farmer and make biscuits and a three-layer chocolate cake and homemade lemonade. They show up and smile a lot and offer everyone some of the food. But no one eats anything.

Less than a week later, they leave Chatham County and move back to Carrboro, and they talk about how odd it was that nobody would eat any of their food and how everyone, including the wife, looked at them as if they hated them. And so they settle back into life in town and play their Paul Robeson records, especially the ones he made in France and Russia, when he got exiled from the United States, and they talk about that day at the store, and all the other things that went on those two months they lived there, and then they get real quiet, trying to figure out what to do next.

August

Jenny Offill

A few days before she died, Becca's mother stopped dreaming. That was what she said at least. The nurse they'd hired claimed this was impossible, that everyone dreamed; she was just too sick to remember them.

But her mother said, no, the dreams had disappeared the moment she went off the morphine. On the morphine, she'd had lovely feverish dreams of bright meadows filled with grass as tall as trees. She'd dreamed she was a balloon that floated high above them. A balloon, Becca thought. Is that how it will be?

The cancer was in her throat by then, and her bones ached even when she rested, but still her mother talked about the future as if it belonged to them. She said, *Soon there will be snow again. Soon we'll play outside and you'll wear your furry boots and your mittens and your hat with the bear ears on it.* She spoke of the snow like a friend who had gone away and was sadly missed but had promised to return to them.

Borrowed time, the nurse called it. Becca had heard her say this to her father once when he came to visit. He didn't live with them anymore. He lived in a crumbling apartment building near school with no garden and only one window. Like someone in a fairy tale who had been sent away. Like someone who'd had a curse put on him. Sometimes Becca got confused and thought he'd left when her mother got sick, but then she remembered that he had left before that. So the curse came after, not before, the terrible thing. The opposite of in the fairy tales.

Before her mother's dreams vanished, she'd told them to Becca each morning as they lay together in bed, Becca sucking on her thumb, her mother worrying a throat lozenge into nothingness.

The dream telling was a happy time wedged between two unhappy ones, the long night with its unfriendly shadows and the long afternoon with her mother's cough worsening until finally her throat was too ragged to speak and she gave up and watched TV instead.

When there was only a little time left, a week at best, she decided to go off the morphine. "I don't want to miss anything," she said. "I want to be awake until the very last minute." But, of course, she slept a little. She couldn't help it. Sometimes her eyes closed against her will and she was gone for a few minutes, an hour even. The first time this happened, Becca waited patiently for her to wake up and tell her what she had dreamed, but when her mother opened her eyes, she said she hadn't seen anything, that there had only been darkness and a low hum like a vacuum cleaner running.

In those last days, her father was always at the house, skulking around making sandwiches no one wanted or peppering the tired nurse with questions. He was always there hovering at the edge of things, but Becca and her mother paid no attention to him. Instead, they huddled under the covers of the big bed and talked on and on, a bright insistent chatter like birds in the morning.

"I'll still talk to you when I'm gone," her mother told her. "But you'll have to listen very carefully because only a whisper of me will be left." She sighed then as if there was more to say, but she didn't have the time for it. On her bedside table was a yellow pad that contained a neatly numbered list. "Explain to Becca," number 5 said.

That was the way her mother was at the end, as calm and organized as she'd always been. The night they came home from the hospital, she'd stayed up late and boxed up all her clothes for charity, then set aside a little store of keepsakes in her closet for Becca: a string of blue beads, her high school yearbook, a recipe for ginger cookies, and the silver spoon and cup she had once fed her with. The note she enclosed said, *Someday you may want these little things. Love always, your mother.*

She'd hoped to organize all the details of her life, but there were too many of them, and by the end the notepad beside her bed was filled with an assortment of things she feared she might go to the grave with: the name and number of Becca's dentist, where her school records were kept, what detergent to wash her blanket in, how to care for the most temperamental of the houseplants. Becca knew these lists were meant for her father, but when they took her mother away, she tore off the pages and hid them under her bed.

LATER, WHEN SHE TALKED about this time, her father claimed that she was too little to remember it, but he was wrong, she remembered everything. She remembered her mother saying she had married too young, that she should have learned French, that the president was no gentleman. And she remembered this: her mother had held her hand in hers and said, *Promise me you'll be happy*, and, not knowing any better, she had said, *Yes*.

·····································

Line

Elizabeth Oliver

Pregnant people rule the world. That's what I'm thinking as I stand in a line eight deep, waiting to go through the self-checkout with my cans of Sheba dog food, the only stuff Max will eat now that he's at home dying and I'm here trying to keep him alive.

"Move your ass," someone whispers from the line beside me, someone short whose head I can barely see over the racks of *Us* and *Star* and *Personality Weekly*. His hair is thinning and red, a washed-out brick faded almost to pink. The skin underneath is mottled and faded too, as if he might emerge from the checkout line and into the full glare of the fluorescent light as a shadowy ghost person, a shell of whoever he used to be.

Dealing with Max was the worst thing going, but I'd been in this same store (only at midnight, less crowded), every month for the past year, picking up yet another pack of tests and a small box of tampons, hedging my bets. I always wore my lucky shoes, my ancient Docs or sometimes my Chucks from high school, as if channeling my younger self could suddenly reverse the aging process. But luck has nothing to do with it, and neither does acupuncture or drinking all the green tea in the whole tea-growing world. A dozen midnights, a dozen negatives. So we've quit. Thirty-seven never seemed too late, until it was.

The ass whisperer is moving ahead more quickly than me and of course I'm jealous. What does he have to get home to anyway—a cussing wife, a couple of bratty teenagers? A sink of dishes he'd never touch, a garage so full of recycling he could read last year's news just by stepping through the door? I picture his house as loud and messy, stuff underfoot and stacked in corners, the TV always on. Not like my house, with NPR on low and Max sleeping all day and my husband barely speaking. I shift my weight from foot to foot, slowly so I don't seem crazy or like I'm about to fall over. I train my face on the magazines in the rack near the whisperer so he won't know I'm watching him. I can see him in my upper right peripheral vision and that will have to do. I can't help but notice all the celebrities on the covers in front of me, rehabbing, expecting, grinning behind huge blind-eyed sunglasses. Baby names like car models, freaky and cool and so annoying. Drugs and movies and money and parties and adopting if things don't work out—or maybe adopting *and* conceiving because sometimes your love is so big you'd buy your own planet to contain it if you could.

I'm moving up, the line is three long now. I don't look to see how many people are behind me because I don't want to know. I don't want that familiar swamped feeling to come, the one that makes me feel stuck in the middle of something I can't get out of. People ahead, people behind, as if I can't step to the side and be clear of them. Ten cans of dog food, tiny tins with pull tabs, all winking in my basket. They are heavier than you'd think, especially when you stand with them for longer than you expect.

The woman in front of me sighs, rests her hand against her hip, braces it against her back like she's been on her feet all day. Maybe she has. Maybe she works somewhere just like this and is totally pissed that she didn't get what she needed before she left instead of on her way home. Or maybe she planned it this way, just couldn't stay at work one second longer once quitting time hit. Makes sense.

The guy is at the checkout now and I stand on tiptoe to see what he has; he's busy with his transaction, so no way he'll look over here at me. I can stare all I want. A small bottle of Clorox, prepackaged bologna not even sliced at the deli. Gross. His hair seems darker from farther away, the pink turning back to brick. His shirt is tucked in because every man over forty tucks his shirt in. Actually, that cutoff may be more like thirty-five, or even thirty-three.

And now I'm up too, because that's how things work. Distract yourself so you're not dizzy with the forward motion; next thing you know it's over and what was the problem to begin with? Hard to remember when I'm fumbling for my wallet, counting out change because that's the mood I'm in today; the mood for cash and not plastic, for watching strange men and not dwelling on dying dogs.

Ten cans of Sheba, all the same, all liver and beef. Strong, smelly, the stuff of life. I wish for the Clorox. I wish for the man to turn around and see me. I wish for things to begin instead of forever ending, over and over and over again.

Miniature

Michael Parker

My first-ever steady job was running the putt-putt place out on the bypass. I was too young to drive and had to get my mother or older sister to drop me off and pick me up, and all too often they'd forget me at night after I'd closed out the cash register and thrown the main switch that lit the course. There was no phone in my plywood shed of an office, no one home to call anyway, and so I would lean against the light pole closest to the road and become gradually a part of it, subsuming its vibrant hum and its dim purplish energy, tremoring when a two-ton blew past on the highway. Late night air cloudy with dust and bugs. Things hurled from high-idling Fords: bad words, bottlecaps, one night a "Knock, knock, who's there?" joke, my weak "Me" followed by a "Me who?" followed by an airborne punchline: one of those cardboard cartons French fries arrive in. After the car peeled off, I snatched up the carton and studied its insides as if it might contain a message for me—*We'll be a few minutes late tonight, just hang tight*—or a ride home. In the murky halo of streetlight cast by my private pole, the carton resembled the shrunken gondola of a hot-air balloon, but where was the helium, and what could I possibly turn up—in this part of town stripped and flattened in the name of development—to use as ballast? I unfolded it, laid it out in the exhaust-blackened grass, examined the grease stains dappling it: dark, unexplored continents bordered by white space of dominant ocean. *Four-fifths of this world is water*, I whispered; *two-thirds of your weight is water weight.* These fluid facts, the deliberate way I offered them to headlights passing, detached me from my light pole and sent me back among the sleeping links of which I was master, manager, pro.

Imaginary putter in hand, I tapped an invisible ball up the

slight grade of number 1, banking off the bowed cornerboard at precisely the spot so many search for but fail to find—I had long since aligned it with a patch of peeling paint—and tightened my grip on the putter as the ball rimmed the cup in a prolonged tease before sinking. Swirling my eyes to follow the ball whizzing round the loop-de-loop on Two, I grew dizzy and lurched like another of the countless drunks who came to play my course on summer nights to where Three's windmill blades churned in the bypass breeze. Like a rock expertly skipped, my ball skimmed the stagnant pondwater of Four. Bogeyed on doglegged Five, double-bogeyed through the prehistoric legs of the plastic brontosaurus straddling Six. A chip into the sandtrap on Seven added strokes I sought to make up for among Eight's grid of miniature stores and houses, its entire tiny town dark and still beneath the shadow of the Haunted Castle hovering at the end of Nine.

Bending to sweep the fairway free of popsicle stick and twig, I balanced my ball meticulously upon the tee, as if ten television cameras had me framed and in focus. I air-clubbed either side of the ball and watched it shiver from the wind of my swing, remembering the way I'd been blown about, moments earlier, by the thunderous wake of tractor-trailers. I closed my eyes I cocked my leg I followed through: across the drawbridge of the black castle rolled my ball, as if summoned supernaturally through the maze of fiberglass battlement. Through the high gargoyled doors it rolled, down into the dungeon it dropped. And although I had been witness to a thousand tantrums thrown by kids who, after a few seconds of deferred impatience, realized that they were not going to get their ball back; although many was the night when I had closed my ears to their wails, which continued, muted but tinny, in the back seats of station wagons gravel-spewing out onto the bypass; even though I knew where the balls went, even though at that very moment my hip pocket bulged with the key to that closet built into the back of the castle where the balls came to rest; *that night* I wanted my ball to not disappear, to pop from one of the parapets or gothic chimneys crowning the castle. I wanted my ball back. I laid across the fairway to mourn its passing. Grinding my cheek into the stubble, I thought I heard, somewhere deep beneath the earth's surface, the rumble of golf balls trapped in a cavern where stalactites punched more dimples in their pocked enamel and moats of lava kept them from spelunking away. Golf ball hell: I heard its rumble while lying there on the bristly carpet of number nine, surrounded by my sleeping kingdom. Out on the highway and into the night roared the cars and trucks of giants, but I could no longer hear them.

. . . .

writers' handbook of editorial and proofreading marks (whepm, 17th Edition)

Peggy Payne

#	insert space
#!@%^	insert space break
IM	insert meaning
x-s	too damn much
tsk	text semi-knowledgeable
wwjd	well, we just don't
otc	overdoing the caps
ill	illustration to come
ssri	sagging story/resuscitation indicated
StAT	stop all this talk
cpr	could possibly revise
wmd	we must discuss
lie	legal issue emerging
A	actionable
perm	need note from author's parents
hdtv	Haute Densitic Tautologic Versionation
ai	artificial intelligence
bs	British style
bdsm	bloody difficult style, mate
jk	just kvetching
sos	sort out symbolism
2—em	second emergency
???	book doctor!!!
M.D.	muddy diction
rn	roaming numerals
-ism	I spy a message
icu	incorrect usage

IV	I veto
DNR	doesn't need revision
EU	editor upset
IEYFL Tower	is English yur frist language?
Shhh	some howlers here, honey
FYI	fancy your inquiring
QUIP	quit using icky puns
IT	incorrect verb tents
STET	stunned editor topples
DOA	dolt of an author!
REJOYCE	go and self-publish, become posthumously immortal

NOW This

Joe Ashby Porter

In cloud without warning a passenger jet flew head-on into the side of a mountain, all fifty-three aboard perishing. Neither pilot had time to register the change of state, lucky for them. The abrupt near-vertical rock face misled the altimeter according to the black box, perhaps in a freak downdraft, with impact shortly before 5:07 A.M., just predawn. When cell chat broke, interlocutors misattributed the static hum to a satellite gap or government scrambling and only began to suspect the truth when after a judicious interval redialing shunted to a voice mailbox. Much vaporized in a fireball. It registered like lightning on nocturnal forest life, and the clap roused many from sleep. Birds directly below fled high branches through incandescent debris that could have compounded the misfortune in a dry season. Kilometers away, birds lifted heads from under wings to peer about, and in an encampment of hunter-gatherers some woke and seemed to hear a spray of biography tailings beneath the hush.

An air-traffic controller caught a blink of anomaly. She networked and within minutes satellite optical feed showed the scintilla. Within hours of daybreak, tut tut two military copters telecast the site. The impassive mountain wore its dark rosette years. Questions of the plane's own radar remained unanswered.

The next morning the destination, Girtly Bonnings, observed a quarter-hour solemn work stoppage, a first although mementos of lesser misfortunes littered the narrow approach between ranges. What with electronic arm-twisting and transfers, the pilot took the fall for having been sucker punched by rock wall. In cushy anonymity his wife and children slipped away to the Society Islands.

147

The unmarried copilot left a condo and a collection of antique decoys to a distant cousin.

The sun-dappled regional capital, longtime conference center, carried on with the following week's international happiness colloquy despite having lost one speaker. Given his obsessive secrecy, little hope remained of reconstructing the calculus he had planned to unveil at the Friday morning plenary session. This pundit's wife and daughter survived when they missed a connecting flight. Eleven other happiness conferees constituted the passenger list's largest grouping.

Sequoia Felver of East Lansing and Berne learned of her heartthrob's mischance via texting from his bereaved dad, a second-generation Iowa hired hand, himself a widower. En route over the pole Sequoia stared at her little screen a good minute as its message sank through blurry denial, this cannot have happened, naw, naw. Tears of rage blurred the darkened cabin. She had dated her cheerful rube barely a year. A loner, Sequoia had seemed to have found a soul mate able to converse after a string of automatons, and now this. Never again his white skin against her black, no kids for backyard hoops with hayseed Cullen for her to scope from her crow's nest office when she glanced up from screens and scratchpads devoted to very old light, Cullen a distance runner at his cornfield school and tech college, the ethanol kid, their meeting in a first-class O'Hare lounge (his standby bump-up delayed at the last minute) scarcely more likely than his untimely end.

The news spread triggering condolence, mourning protocol, and investigation, and thinned as it propagated through its own short life, with restrained international broadband listing casualties and offering obits of the happiness theoretician and also a mid-list spinner of young adult sports narrative whose house toyed with dedicating a fitness center to their departed author lost just before the guilty-pleasure groundswell, adults steeping themselves in comforting scope and enlarged typeface, market share shifted from "adult" text.

Sequoia never married, although she sampled the occasional hookup. Her grief over Cullen eased with time, and she came to understand that, after all, all might have been for the best, at least for her, she who comparatively undistracted acquired glistening professional distinctions despite a younger colleague's having stolen credit for a breakthrough.

On the tenth anniversary of Cullen's demise, Sequoia made virtual love with him exactly as if he had missed the fateful flight, nor had aged a day. They said scarcely a word, and before their climaxes she guessed rightly that she would be denied repetition even should she seek it. Menopause soon followed, a seeming corporeal adieu until she found herself virtually pregnant and, thinking back, couldn't recall taking precautions. The quick pregnancy culminated in a birth so painless as not to disturb the new mother's early morning sleep. She named her offspring Slade, unable to determine its gender.

From early on Slade disappeared for days at a time like a cat. In skin color as generally the child resembled its mother more than its father, although the cheekbone freckles came from Cullen. Sequoia took in stride her child's accelerated maturation and how with adolescence Slade's gender precipitated into a chameleonic either-or that could flip with no more warning than a certain faraway look.

"Mother?"

"Yes, dear?" Spring Saturday, noonish in a quiet Swiss park, ferns, birdsong, scudding cloudlets.

"If you'd found yourself pregnant after the crash, would I have a sib? They say tests show parents give firstborns the lion's share of attention."

Sequoia mused. "Love's different though. Anyway it wasn't in the cards. With the actual act, your father and I always availed ourselves of protection. Redundant protection, in fact."

"Mustn't have seemed necessary conceiving me."

"Little we knew, luckily. More than luckily."

Life on Mars

Denise Rickman

When I was a kid I really thought I could be an astronaut. We used to practice for the end of the world, you know, duck-and-cover, hands over your head and the bombs will miss you. I didn't last long in Catholic school, but I can tell you even the nuns rolled their eyes at that shit. And I didn't want to die, so I made this deal with God: I'd be real good if He'd just let me fly a spaceship. I'd learn my times tables and wear a bowtie in church and stop calling Oliver Martin "pudgebutt," even when he deserved it, and He'd make me an astronaut so that when the bombs started falling, I could get in my spaceship and head for Mars or the moon, wherever I felt like going. It wasn't entirely selfish, I was going to take my parents and Michael Samson from Little League and my Grandma Judy.

I didn't tell anyone about my genius plan because I figured it would be worth extra points if no one knew why I was being so lovable and virtuous all of a sudden. They'd wonder, of course, but they couldn't fully appreciate it, not until the world started ending, when I'd swoop in with my spaceship and save the day. And Dad would go, "Danny, you really are a good kid. Can you ever forgive us for doubting you?"

And I'd say, "Oh, you guys," like a kid on TV, and we'd all hug, and the studio audience would go, "Awwww."

I thought I was so fucking smart. It never occurred to me to wonder what we would do in that spaceship, alone with each other for the rest of our lives.

When the world didn't end, I still wanted to be an astronaut. Up until I was in eighth grade, which is really too old for that shit, and I saw this TV show about space, and how no one ever goes to the moon anymore, just around in circles. I thought, why bother?

Also, it was around this time that I figured out that NASA probably doesn't let fags fly the space shuttle, which is totally something Roger would say. Except he wouldn't call us fags, just guys that are into other guys or something self-righteous and boring like that. He's nineteen, the same as me, but he's so earnest all the time. He gets huffy every time we go out, like, "Danny, is the lipstick really necessary? And why are you wearing a bra? Are you out of clean shirts? Why do you have a bra?" And OK, I am wearing a bra, but it's not like I'm stuffing it, and it's pretty subdued, except for the sequin straps. I just don't want people to ignore me. Is that so wrong? "You're wearing a bra," Roger says, resigned. "Are you doing that to your hair on *purpose*? Do you even own a comb? You can always borrow mine, you know." Roger would bring a comb to an orgy.

I could kind of almost love him, except I hate how he keeps trying to make me into this tragic little gay orphan so his upwardly mobile, boring-ass friends can go, "Wow, Roger, that's so sad. He's so brave." When really I took a bus to Grandma Judy's house when I was fourteen and just didn't go back. It wasn't some earth-shattering ordeal. They're still my parents, and if we haven't spoken in almost a year, what would we say? The stupid part of my astronaut daydream wasn't believing in God, or that the world would end, or that I could do anything about it. It wasn't even the spaceship. It was believing that I would take them with me when I escaped. There's no room for them here.

An Afternoon, No wind

David Rowell

A striking, big-boned woman runs back and forth trying to fly a kite. She is surprisingly eager, considering there is no wind today. There is not enough of a breeze to sail the gum wrapper off the bench I'm sitting on. She darts tirelessly across the park as the kite drags behind her like a little dog. Every so often the kite lifts off the ground, though no higher than her head, and that's only because she is a fast runner. This goes on for an hour.

I'm supposed to be helping my ex-girlfriend move her tanning bed into the spare room. But when the woman with the kite throws her arms up in an almost vaudevillian show of disgust, I get up, stiff from the wooden slats, and walk over to her. She isn't aware of me until I am close enough to touch her.

"Tough day for kites," I say.

We look at each other, and for a few seconds neither of us seems sure what to do. I back up a step or two. I am suddenly confused and can't remember if I have spoken yet or just thought about what I might say. *Tough day for kites?*

"Je ne comprendsabsolument pas cequevousdites." I know it's French, but I don't speak a word of it. Watching her earlier, it didn't occur to me that she wasn't American, but up close I can see the faint olive glow of her skin, the slightly pouty curl of her lips. I consider turning around, leaving her alone, but there is something helpless about her and her shiny but now damaged triangular kite. I point to the kite, then to the sky. I blow a deep breath and shake my head no.

"No wind," I say slowly, so slowly that I am keenly aware of how my lips feel when they move. "There is no wind."

We stand another moment in silence, as the strangled cry of taxi horns and someone's high-pitched laughter and the rusty churn of a nearby bicycle chain play off each other like jazz musicians. Behind the woman a mass of clouds forms a penguin, then a penguin on skates. She says something—something abrupt, like an order—and points to the kite. She points at me, then to the kite again. I reach down to pick it up.

"Oui," she says.

I raise the kite slowly over my head, arching my brow to say, *Is this OK? Is this what you want?* She doesn't indicate one way or another. Out of the corner of my eye I notice that two older women who are dressed for the tundra have stopped to watch.

She backs up and lets some string out, all the while staring into my eyes so intensely that I am afraid to look away. She nods her head once, the way mob bosses in movies indicate their willingness to listen first, before killing. Then she turns and starts sprinting, divots of grass spraying from her heels. The kite jerks out of my hand and immediately sinks, not quite hitting the ground because, as I say, she's fast. Her ponytail thrashes behind her like a fish pulled into a boat.

She goes probably thirty yards before she looks up at the speckled sky, where she expects the kite to be. Her sturdy legs slow to a gallop, which causes the kite to touch down with feathery impact. The sad sight provokes her to grunt from the diaphragm and kick at the ground with such force that she nearly falls over. Her large frame heaves in and out. She yells something at either me or the kite (the literal translation might be, "What a piece of crap are you!"). I point up at the sky again and shake my head.

When she finishes winding up the string, she puts the kite back in my hands. I notice two small but distinct moles above her right eye. She catches me looking and balls up her face like a fist. She gives me an earful about something, to which I shrug and smile, though not with my teeth.

All afternoon we do this. And every time we try, I can tell that she expects it to go differently. Sometimes I shake my head in mock disbelief. Other times I grab a handful of grass and launch it into the air, as if that might tell us something. Once I try to hand the kite back to her and reach for the string, thinking she might appreciate the break. But she shakes her head in a frenzy, the way monkeys do in TV commercials, and holds the string behind her back. She tries running harder and for longer. If I hold the kite up with my arms even slightly bent, she refuses to start running. When yet another attempt fails, she violently reels the kite in. As we get ready again, she sucks some air into her locomotive lungs, then gives me the signal to release.

By now the sun has melted to the bottom of the sky, leaving behind a fiery red glaze. People walk by with their necks turned at awkward angles, their mouths agape with wonder. My French companion is still for the first time all day. We stand there a while, just a few feet apart, but it's hard to believe we've spent the entire afternoon together. If I ran over the hill and brought back two sno-cones, I wonder if she would even recognize me.

The man at the pretzel cart is folding down his umbrella. I imagine a big wind suddenly sweeping through the park and lifting the umbrella up over the trees, the man kicking wildly in the air as he tries to hang on. When I look over again at my partner in aeronautics, it takes me a moment to realize that she is tearing the kite up. She grips it in her muscular arms and splits it down the middle. She yanks out the sticks of the frame, fumbling with them until she snaps them over her knee. Then, with lips moving but making no sound, she grabs the tail with both hands and tries to twist it off, but she loses patience with it and is content to leave it a thin, raggedy string. Her hands are a frenzied blur of methodical destruction, though her face has an even, almost serene expression. When she is finally satisfied, she bundles up the remains and hands them to me. Instinctively I reach out to cradle the wreckage.

She lumbers toward the wrought iron entrance of the park, past the statue of George Washington on his horse, past a little boy trying to step on his balloon, which keeps darting out from under his foot. She steps directly in front of a stretch limousine so that it has to slam on brakes; still, the driver senses enough not to honk. She mows through the streets with an elephantine grace and does not fade from view until well after the darkness settles in.

I COULD GO OVER THIS AGAIN, say at what point this, then that, but it would more or less come out the same. And yet there is something that I can't account for, even now: In my arms the kite felt like a bouquet of flowers.

The Teachers' Lounge

John Rowell

While other fifth-grade children at Coble Road Elementary busied themselves with thoughts of science projects, Little League games, food fights, and Saturday morning cartoons, Ritchie Upchurch pondered endlessly what went on behind the closed door of the school's teachers' lounge.

At recess, while standing on the sidelines during a game of dodgeball, Ritchie told his friend Arlie Blevins: "When they're in there, all by themselves with the door closed, they make secret plans on how they're going to flunk us! The whole time they're in there, they say, 'Let's see . . . who's gonna repeat fifth grade next year?'"

At the art sink, as he and Billy Lindsay stood alone washing paint brushes, he whispered: "They do wild things in there. They smoke opium cigarettes, like in *The Arabian Nights*. I've seen them, when the door opens. And they drink. They drink liquor drinks! And then they come to class drunk. Drunk like skunks!"

"I don't believe you," Billy said. "You make stuff up."

Then Ritchie added: "They have a *bar* in there. And the janitor is the bartender!"

Eventually, after one of Ritchie's daily sermonettes on life in the teachers' lounge, the boy who had formed his captive audience of one would soon find a reason to run off with some of the other kids to grab a few extra minutes of kickball on the playground for the remainder of the lunch period or the ten-minute morning break. Ritchie would choose instead to find a reason to loiter in the main hallway near the door on which the words "TEACHERS' LOUNGE" had been drawn years ago with old-fashioned stencils and filled in with black tempera paint. Conveniently, a water fountain stood in an alcove right next to the lounge; whenever a teacher approached, Ritchie would dive for more water, so as not to attract attention.

IN MOMENTS WHEN Ritchie could get his ear close enough to the door, he would hear snatches of conversation: he'd catch the name of an occasional student being bandied about before making a sudden dive for the water fountain. *Joey Robbins*, *Porter Shea*, *Travis Beard*. He couldn't get all the details, but he was sure what he heard had to do with the fact that each boy would be flunked out by year's end. Perhaps the teachers had decided that Porter, who, in the second grade, had tried to kill the class gerbil by feeding it M&M's, should be sent to Juvenile Correction . . . or perhaps up to Dix Hill in Raleigh, where Ritchie knew all the crazy people in North Carolina eventually had to go.

One day, as Ritchie hovered between the lounge door and the water fountain, he very clearly heard Mrs. Lenora Peet use the word "divorced" in a sentence (as she always told students to do with spelling words). In a random opening of the door, he glimpsed a perfect, almost spotlit view of her as she blew the word out with an upward puff of her opium cigarette: "I hear they're getting *divorced!*" she said, and the word practically hovered in the smoky air, like in a balloon in the Sunday funnies, until the door shut just as quickly again in his face and he ducked back to the water fountain.

RITCHIE DESPERATELY LONGED to be invited into the teachers' lounge—he imagined himself to be the first student in Coble Road Elementary history to be afforded such a privilege. On that day, he would wear his Sunday school shirt and his favorite blue clip-on tie, which featured a picture of a water-skiing couple holding up a banner that read: "North Carolina: Variety Vacationland!" He would be invited to sit on the couch between Mrs. Peet and Miss Hambrick as Mr. Thaddeus Lattimore worked the mimeograph machine. Ritchie would watch his muscles rippling under his shirt as he turned the hand crank with one hand while hefting a big brown beer bottle in the other, resembling a cheerful, handsome john rowell

man in a TV ad over whom ladies swooned and fainted. Surely Mr. Teague Buford would offer to make Ritchie a drink at the bar, the bar that was, naturally, tucked into a far corner, out of sight from the hallway. Over the bar, "TEACHERS' LOUNGE" spelled out in blinking red neon lights, a big improvement, in Ritchie's mind, over stencils and tempera paint. Miss Hambrick and Mrs. Peet would also be knocking back cocktails—high noon on a typical school day!—while grading reading quizzes and spelling tests and trading vicious, intimate gossip between them.

"Did you see what Travis Beard's trampy mama wore to Back to School PTA?" Mrs. Peet would ask both Ritchie and Miss Hambrick. "Why, I wouldn't have worn that to *Mardi Gras*, much less to meet my child's teachers! Nothing but trash on parade!"

Mrs. Peet would deposit her cigarette butt—the tip of it gone cardinal red from her lipstick—into an ashtray made of multistacked, glued-together popsicle sticks (a donation from Miss Winnifred Seeley's fourth- and fifth-grade art classes, which Ritchie helped to make). Ritchie would excuse himself and make his way over to the bar to freshen his Shirley Temple, and there, under the neon sign, other teachers would be perched on barstools.

"Why, Ritchie Upchurch!" they would say, leaning into him over piles of carelessly graded English themes, now stained with sloshed bourbon. "How fabulous of you to come to the lounge. Tell us . . . do you know who's getting . . . *a divorce?*"

One day after school, after most of the other children had gone home, Ritchie stood waiting in the hallway for his father to pick him up. It was raining, so he chose to wait inside.

"Ritchie Upchurch?"

It was his art teacher, Miss Seeley, carrying a large cardboard box. "Ritchie, would you mind opening the door for me, please? I need to drop this in the teachers' lounge."

Ritchie's heart suddenly began to beat faster and his mouth went dry. Uncharacteristically, he didn't speak, only moved to push the door open instead. He pushed it all the way, taking himself in with it. Once inside, he looked around at beige walls decorated with posters of famous children's books and signs that said things

158

like "Reading Is Fundamental." On the shelves below the windows, textbooks and files were stacked in an orderly fashion; the teachers' mailbox slots bordered the end of a bookcase. The Coke machine light had been turned off, and a few magazines were scattered around on work tables: *NEA Bulletin, Teacher's Guide to My Weekly Reader*, old copies of *Jack and Jill*. In a corner, Mr. Buford worked to repair a table leg; Miss Hambrick, seated at a work table, sipped from a coffee mug as she graded papers. The whole room radiated quiet, like church, save for the buzz of the fluorescent lights, and the air smelled of coffee and mimeograph ink. Ritchie looked around, blank-faced and blinking.

"Thank you, Ritchie," Miss Seeley said, holding the door open for him to leave.

TWENTY MINUTES LATER, his father pulled up in his rusty Ranchero Deluxe. Ritchie had gotten used to the lateness; his father was the one who picked him up now. A month ago, Ritchie's mother had left the house one afternoon, saying only that she was going to stay at her sisters' place for a while down in South Carolina. One thing Ritchie missed was that she always picked him up from school on time.

"Learn anything today?" his father asked, as he pulled the Ranchero out of the parking lot.

"No."

"Nothing?"

Ritchie looked back at the windows of the teachers' lounge; the Venetian blinds were pulled up haphazardly all the way across. The fluorescent lights had been turned off.

"No," he said, turning his head around. "Not much."

The Conductress

Deborah Seabrooke

"Babbo, vieni da noi," my daughter said on the phone. ("Dad, come see us.") "Make the trip. Your grandson is finally engaged and we'll celebrate."

The train cuts through fields outside Torino.

I can't concentrate on my book. Instead all I see is the back of the boy's head. At the previous stop he told me to move, this boy with battered schoolbooks, stinking of cigarettes. We compared tickets. I pulled my suitcase off the rack. Bumping down the aisle, I discovered my proper seat.

THE CONDUCTRESS ENTERS THE CAR, gripping the handlebars of a bike. She yells at an old man who follows right behind her: "Dai!" ("Move!") "Don't worry. I've got your bike! Move!" She stops at the empty seat next to me and asks, "May I leave my bag here?" I nod yes.

"Dovete scendere subito!" she continues yelling. ("You must get off this train right now!") "Move!"

I tell myself, if the boy had not made me move earlier, then the conductress would have shown me my proper seat and not so nicely. She with her bag and deep honey eyes that gave me a half-second's throb in my trousers.

Up the aisle, the boy has fallen asleep against the window. The old man and his bike wait with the conductress in the windy vestibule between this car and the one ahead. The wheels screech as we brake for the next stop. She won't have him riding her train for free.

Her bag carries everything a conductress needs. The buckle is undone and my fingers climb inside: schedules, ticket punch, a pad with delicate carbons, a side pocket, a hair clasp. I take that.

The Assistant D.A.

Dave Shaw

After half of a marathon interrogation, I have fallen in love with the assistant D.A. It doesn't bode well for me, of course, but I simply can't help myself. She has to struggle, it seems, to keep her lips from their natural inclination to part when she has nothing to say. I have to struggle to refrain from confessing to grand larceny, though I've only been jailed for petty theft. Somehow, I do manage to keep my mouth clamped, and back to jail I go to await my justice. It is a justice that, the assistant D.A. assures me, is quite swift around these parts. With or without my cooperation.

Within a few days, I can't stand my jail cell, alone there without her. I walk in circles. I do my jumping jacks. I spit through the bars at marks on the tiles. Quite frankly, I'm dying for her, for her tight skirts and sly, noncommittal smiles. In my hours of isolation and boredom, I convince myself that she and her marvelous lips will give me a break. Because, I convince myself, *she* has fallen for *me*. Hadn't our session before been a little extensive merely for questioning about a petty theft? Hadn't her quiet shifting in her chair been a fairly overt attempt to flirt? In the long lonely quiet of my cell, her motives have become clear to me. I arrange to have a special meeting with her. Alone.

At our meeting she sits across the table from me, resting a finger behind her ear under a few unruly strands of blond hair. She says nothing. I look into her green eyes, and suddenly I know that I am right. These wonderful sunbursts shifting in her irises, adjusting, compensating for the shadows of clouds passing outside the gridded window, tell me that she, too, *is* indeed in love with me. I confess it all. The petty theft, a stolen credit card ring, a dubious paint and body shop I ran eleven years ago. I mention the income

161

tax evasion and the laundering, the larceny and embezzlement, the quote-unquote *pawn* shop, the numbers and false futures that I sold to a few doctors, the telemarketing schemes, even the two dot-com start-ups with the imaginary backers from Boston. She allows her lips to part.

The entire episode is quite cleansing, so cleansing in fact that I begin making up crimes to confess. We're in love and I'm taking advantage of the situation, all the while absolved of everything by the understanding shining so greenly in her eyes. When I'm finally done, I feel the renewal that only a total confession to a lover can bring.

She uncrosses her legs. She stands a little shakily. Then she whispers the obvious to me. "I love you," she says, pushing a few more wisps of that golden hair behind her ear.

"I know," I say. "I know." She leaves and we agree not to say good-bye.

A day and a half later, my justice is meted out, swiftly, just as she promised at our first meeting. She, in that cute way of hers, waves the transcripts of my confessions and asks the judge to throw the book at me, without even once looking my way. I receive seven nonconcurrent sentences of varying lengths and obligations, and I marvel at how truly wonderful it is to be in love again.

The Cottage-Mover

Bland Simpson

Fifty or sixty years ago, my second cousin once removed's uncle by marriage, Uncle John Ferebee, was a legendary cottage-mover on the Outer Banks of North Carolina. He specialized in sliding cottages westward, back away from the encroaching ocean, though he also moved them north and south up and down the beach. Over on Roanoke Island, any number of homes in Manteo now stand on foundations they were not built upon, thanks to this man's work. There was nothing he couldn't move—why, I believe he once moved a small hotel!

Down on Hatteras Island, back in the 1950s when the moving of the Cape Hatteras Lighthouse first got talked about, they even consulted with him to see how he would do it, and, though it wasn't till 1999 that the light retreated from the Atlantic, old-timers say that some of the cottage-mover's suggestions and methods from forty years earlier were put to use.

Uncle John was extremely well known, *famous* even, as the man who could move anything.

Famous, that is, in Dare County and parts of eastern Hyde and southern Currituck Counties, and probably not unknown over in swampy Tyrrell. Yet once that we know of, his fame transcended the Carolina sound country and made it all the way up to Manhattan.

An old lady from Manteo decided she needed to take a trip and go see New York City one time in her life. So she got there and signed up for the Gray Line "Historic Sites" Tour right away. First place they went was to see the Old Dutch House, a little two-story affair down on Wall Street dwarfed by the towers of commerce, and after the tour guide's spiel, the old lady from Manteo was unimpressed and said from the back of the crowd, "We got one of these back home."

The tour guide was peeved but held his tongue. And then they went over to St. Mark's Place and looked at the beautiful commercial buildings along 2nd Avenue, the Italianate details of the roofs and windows, and the little old lady thought about the antique buildings in downtown Manteo and said, a little louder this time, "We got some of these back home."

Then they drifted down to South Street Seaport and studied the historic ships there, and the old lady, reminded of all the weathered boats in Shallowbag Bay there at Manteo, said firmly: "We got some of these back home!"

And so it went, all through the whole four-hour tour, the tour guide getting more and more steamed by the old Manteo lady's refrain but never responding, till they finally reached the last site of the day: the Empire State Building. They went up to the observation deck, and the tour guide pointed out features of the New York skyline, showed them all the yellow cabs in the world down below. And then, tapping on the great skyscraper's side, he preempted the little old lady from Manteo, saying, "Well, madam, I know you don't have one of *these* back home."

"No," she said. "But we got somebody can move it."

sex, love, death, sex, high school

Lee Smith

The house I grew up in was one of a row of houses strung along a narrow riverbottom like a string of beads. We were not allowed to play in the river because they washed coal in it, upstream. Its water ran deep and black between the mountains that rose like walls on either side of us, rocky and thick with trees.

My mother came from the flat exotic eastern shore of Virginia and swore that the mountains gave her migraine headaches. Mama was always lying down on the sofa, all dressed up. But there was no question that she loved my father, a mountain man she had chosen over the well-bred Arthur Banks of Richmond, a "fellow who went to the University of Virginia and never got over it," according to Daddy. Mama suffered from ideas of aristocracy herself. Every night she would fix a nice supper for Daddy and me, then bathe and put on a fresh dress and high heels and her bright red lipstick, named "Fire and Ice," and then sit in anxious dismay while the hour grew later and later, until Daddy finally left his dime store and came home.

By that time the food had dried out to something crunchy and unrecognizable, so Mama would cry when she opened the oven door, but Daddy would eat it all anyway, swearing it was the most delicious food he'd ever put in his mouth, staring hard at Mama all the while. Frequently my parents would then leave the table abruptly, feigning huge yawns and leaving me to turn out all the lights. I'd stomp around the house and do this resentfully, both horrified and thrilled at the thought of them upstairs behind their closed door.

I myself was in love with my best friend's father, three houses down the road. Mr. Owens had huge dark soulful eyes, thick black

165

hair, a mustache that dropped down on either side of his mouth, and the prettiest singing voice around. Every night after supper, he'd sit out in his garden by the river and play his guitar and sing for us and every other kid in the neighborhood who'd gather around to listen.

Mr. Owens played songs like "Wayfaring Stranger" and "The Alabama Waltz." He died the year we were thirteen, from an illness described as "romantic fever." Though later I would learn that the first word was actually "rheumatic," in my own mind it remained "romantic fever," an illness I associated with those long summer evenings when my beloved Mr. Owens played the old sad songs while lightning bugs rose like stars from the misty weeds along the black river and right down the road—three houses away—my own parents were kissing like crazy as night came on.

THE LINK BETWEEN love and death intensified when my MYF group (that's Methodist Youth Fellowship) went to Myrtle Beach, where we encountered many exotic things such as pizza pie and northern boys smoking cigarettes on the boardwalk. Our youth leader, who was majoring in drama at a church school, threw our cigarettes into the surf and led us back onto the sandy porch of Mrs. Fickling's Boardinghouse for an emergency lecture on Petting.

"A nice girl," she said dramatically, "does not Pet. It is cruel to the boy to allow him to Pet because he has no control over himself. He is just a boy. It is all up to the girl. If she allows the boy to Pet her, then he will become excited, and if he cannot find relief, then the poison will all back up into his organs causing pain—and sometimes *death*!" She spat out the words.

We drew back in horror and fascination.

OF COURSE IT WASN'T LONG before I found myself in the place where I'd been headed all along: the front seat of a rusty old pickup, heading up a mountain on a dark gravel road with a wild older boy—let's call him Wayne—whom I scarcely knew but had secretly adored for months. This was not the nice boy I'd been dating, the football star/student government leader who'd carried my books around from class to class all year and held my hand in study hall. My friends were all jealous of me for attracting such a nice boyfriend; even my mother approved. But, though he dutifully pressed his body against mine at dances in the gym whenever they played "The Twelfth of Never," our song, it just wasn't happening. That fiery hand did not clasp my vitals as it did in *Jane Eyre* whenever Jane encountered Mr. Rochester.

So I had seized my chance when Wayne asked me if I'd like to ride around sometime. "You bet!" I'd said so fast it startled him. "I'd love to!" Wayne was a big, slow-talking boy with long black hair that fell down into his handsome, sullen face. He wore a ring of keys on his belt and a pack of cigarettes rolled up in the sleeve of his T-shirt. I admired his style as much as I admired his family — or lack of family, I should say, for he lived with his uncle out in a trailer near the county line. Wayne smoked, drank, and played in a band with grownup men. He was always on the Absentee Hot List, and soon he'd be gone for good, headed off to Nashville with a shoebox full of songs.

We jolted up the rutted road through dense black woods. My mother would have died if she'd known where I was. But she didn't. Nobody did.

I was determined to Pet with Wayne even if it killed him.

Finally we emerged onto a kind of dark, windy plateau, an abandoned strip-mine site on top of the mountain. He drove right up to the edge, a sheer drop. I caught my breath. On the mountainside below us were a hundred coke ovens sending their fiery blasts like giant candles straight up into the sky. It was like the pit of hell itself, but beautiful. It was the most beautiful thing I'd ever seen. For some reason I started crying.

"Aw," he said. He screwed the top off a mason jar and gave me a drink that burned all the way down. "You know what?" He pulled me over toward him. He smelled like smoke, like alcohol, like the woods.

"What?" I said into the sleeve of his blue jeans jacket.

"They was a boy killed in one of them ovens last month—fell in, or throwed himself in, nobody ever did know which."

"Was there?" I scooted closer.

"Yep, it was a boy from over on Paw Paw, had a wife and two little babies. Gone in the twinkling of an eye, just like it says in the Bible." He snapped his fingers. "Right down there," he said into my hair.

"That's awful." I shuddered, turning up my face for his kiss, while below us the coke ovens burned like a hundred red fountains of death and I felt the fiery hand clutch my vitals for good.

Finally, I thought.

Romantic fever.

······································

cars

June Spence

This was not my father's Oldsmobile. It was my mother's: a white 1978 Cutlass Supreme with a powder blue vinyl top and matching velveteen interior. She took possession of it as part of their separation agreement, and she held onto it for years, just as she'd held fast to the only other car of their marriage she'd had the foresight to register in her own name: a mustard Pinto station wagon with faux wood panels.

Cars in my father's name tended to disappear before the oil needed changing. In the early days of my parents' courtship and marriage, he'd gone through a 1947 Chevy panel truck, a Studebaker of unknown vintage, a green Galaxy, a Pontiac convertible, and two '49 Fords, one of which he watched burn past salvation in the driveway after dropping a lit cigarette into the engine block. The '49 Ford lacked the insurance to fund its replacement, so my father's behavior was somewhat mysterious. He has since described to me a sort of Buddhist capitulation upon losing the cigarette, an accident he decided not to thwart.

Perhaps he sensed the ceaseless stream of cars that would continue to flow through his life. Here and just as swiftly gone was the sleek black Dart of my parents' honeymoon, gone the cheery red Beetle and yellow Karmann Ghia of my toddlerhood, gone the beach-gritty camper van and the wee Toyota truck that veered and hauled without complaint. So ephemeral perhaps I only dreamed the motorcycle one wind-buffeted trip around the block clinging to my father's broad back, my head lolling inside the adult-sized helmet like the clapper of a bell.

Except for the conflagration of the '49 Ford, my father tended to dispose of his vehicles through frequent, compulsive trade-ins.

And as my parents' incomes rose, he began buying new and trading up. The '78 Oldsmobile Cutlass Supreme represented a pinnacle in our fortunes: we'd moved from compact German and Japanese models to big new domestic cars that belied the fuel crisis, finally settling on this imposing American sedan.

For a time the stately Cutlass rested uneasily in the driveway alongside our decidedly homelier Pinto wagon. The Pinto had dragged our sweating carcasses wherever we had cousins to stay with in the summer: Virginia, Florida, Texas. It did not shirk at hauling dogs, whether shedding or sick, or children in wet bathing suits eating chocolate ice cream. But the Cutlass was meant for finer things. Its fussy velveteen seats did not fold down in the back so my sister and I could sprawl indolently among puzzles and coloring books; neither could they tolerate pets or spillage. In the Cutlass we were meant to smoothly traverse the countryside, the FM stereo emitting decorous tones as we chatted companionably.

It was a car, a lifestyle, my father aspired to, but it wasn't one we could sustain. Nor could he trade it away with impunity; my mother laid claim to the Olds when they split and bequeathed to him the Pinto wagon. He swapped it at once for a Honda Civic, that spartan car of bachelors and practicality, and not long after that a sporty two-seater, a Pontiac Fiero, that could squire his girlfriend or one daughter but never both.

I remember my mother creeping out early, still in her foamy pink robe and scuffs, to crank the Cutlass on frosty mornings and let it warm up while she got ready for work. She'd retained all the trappings, the house, car, and kids, and it took all of these plus every ounce of her strength to deflect whatever pity she sensed might be directed her way in the early days of the divorce. With her travel mug of black coffee wobbling next to her on the plush seat and low-tar cigarette smoldering in the gilded ashtray, she'd steady dark glasses on the bridge of her nose, tilt the sun visor, and ease the Cutlass out of the cul-de-sac and into the press and merge of cars until she slipped onto the loop that orbited the city.

My mother drove that car until she paid it off, and then she went and bought another one just as fast and fine, and nobody helped her to do it.

. . . .

The Everlasting Light

Elizabeth Spencer

Kemp Donahue was standing at the window one December afternoon, watching his daughter Jessie come up the walk. Without reason or warning, his eyes filled with tears.

What on earth?

She came closer, books in her old frayed satchel, one sock slipped down into the heel of her shoe, looking off and thinking and smiling a little. Kemp scrubbed the back of his hand across his eyes.

Why had he cried? Something to do with Jessie?

Jessie was not at all pretty (long face, uneven teeth, thin brown hair), and though Sheila, Kemp's trim and lovely looking wife, never mentioned it, they both knew how she felt about it. But what did pretty mean?

Jessie, now in the kitchen rummaging in the fridge, was into everything at school. She sold tickets to raffles, she tried out for basketball. Once rejected for the team, she circulated announcements for the games and lobbied for door prizes.

Kemp came to the kitchen door. "What's new, honey?"

"Oh, nothing. Choir practice."

Mentioning it, she turned and grinned, ear to ear. ("Smile," her mother admonished. "Don't grin.")

Jessie loved choir practice. Nonchurchgoers, the parents had decided a few years back it would be good to send Jessie to Sunday school a few times. To their surprise, she liked it. She went back and back. She colored pictures, she came home and told Bible stories, she loved King David, she loved Joshua, she loved Jesus, she loved Peter and Paul. Sheila and Kemp listened to some things they didn't even know. ("Good Lord," said Sheila, hearing about the walls of Jericho.)

Elizabeth spencer

"Choir practice," Kemp repeated.

Sheila was out for the evening at one of her meetings. She was a secretary at the history department at the university. Twilight was coming on. "Are you eating enough?" asked Kemp. He wanted to talk to his daughter, just him and her. What did he want to say? It was all in his throat, but he couldn't get it out. "Honey . . . ," he began. Jessie looked up at him, munching a tuna sandwich in the side of one jaw. ("Don't chew like that," Sheila said.) "Honey . . . ," Kemp said again. He did not go on.

After a lonely dinner at the cafeteria, Kemp drove up to the church and wandered around. The churchyard was dark, but light was coming from the windows, and the sound of singing as well was coming out. It was very sweet and clear, the sound of young voices. At the church, there were two morning services. At the early, nine o'clock service, the young choir sang. At the 11:15 service, the grown-up choir took over, the best in town, so people said.

Kemp did not go in the church but stood outside. He crept closer to the church wall to listen. They were singing Christmas carols. He knew "Silent Night" and "Jingle Bells" and that silly one about Rudolph. But as for the others, they had a familiar ring, sure enough, and he found himself listening for Jessie's voice and thinking he heard it.

O little town of Bethlehem,
How still we see thee lie.
Above thy deep and dreamless sleep
The silent stars go by.

Still in thy dark streets shineth
The everlasting light . . .

"Everlasting light . . ." That stuck in Kemp's mind. He kept repeating it. He strained to hear the rest. What came after little town and dreamless sleep and silent stars? He was leaning against the wall, puzzling out the words until the song faded, and he could even hear the rap of the choir director's wand, and his voice too. Another song?

Kemp looked up. A strange woman was approaching the church and was looking at him. She was stooped over and white-haired, and every bit of her said he had no business leaning up against the church wall on a December night. He straightened, smiled, and spoke to her and hastened away, pursued by strains of

Away in a manger, no crib for a bed,
The little Lord Jesus . . .

At breakfast the next morning, Kemp said, "Tell me, Jessie, what's that Christmas carol that says something about 'the everlasting light' . . . ?"

Jessie told him. She knew the whole thing. She was about to start on "Joy to the World," but her mother stopped her. "Your eggs are getting cold as ice," she pointed out firmly.

"Why don't we all go to church tomorrow," Kemp proposed. "We can hear them all sing."

Sheila valued her Sunday sleep more than average, but she finally agreed, and the Donahues, arriving in good time, listened to all sorts of prayers and Bible readings and music and a sermon too. Everyone was glad to see them. Jessie wore her little white robe.

"Well, now," said Kemp when they reached home. "Maybe that's how Sunday ought to be."

Sheila looked at him in something like alarm.

Sheila was from New England, a graduate of one of those schools people spoke of with awe. Kemp was Virginia born, and though it seemed odd for a southern family, he had never been encouraged to attend church. Kemp did audits for a Piedmont chain of stores selling auto parts; he drove a good bit to various locations. Driving alone, he found himself repeating, "dark streets . . . the everlasting light. . . ." He especially liked that last. Didn't it just *sound* everlasting? Then, because they didn't have one, he had sneaked and borrowed Jessie's Bible. It took him a long time, but he found the story and relished the phrases: "The glory of the Lord shone round about them. . . ." *That's great!* thought Kemp.

One week more and it would be the weekend of Christmas.

Sheila said at breakfast, "Now, Jessie, you're certainly going to the Christmas party at school?"

"I have to go to choir practice," said Jessie.

"No, you do not," said Sheila. "It won't matter to miss one time. Miss Fagles rang up and said she especially wanted you. There's some skit you wrote for the class."

"They did that last year," said Jessie. "Anyway, I told Mr. Jameson I'd come."

"Then tell him you can't."

"I don't want to," said Jessie.

Sheila put down her napkin. She appealed to Kemp. "I am not going to have this," she said.

Kemp realized he was crucial, but he said it anyway. "Let her go where she wants to."

Sheila went upstairs in a fury. She had always wanted a pretty daughter who had lots of boyfriends begging for her time. "She's impossible," she had once muttered to Kemp.

Even the Donahues usually attended church on Christmas and Easter, and this year was no exception. The church was packed and fragrant with boughs of cedar. They heard carols and once more the stories of shepherds and angels read from the pulpit. They heard the choir and told Jessie later how proud they were of the way she sang. "But you couldn't hear me for everybody else," said Jessie.

It was at dinner a day or so later that she said: "The funniest thing happened the last night we practiced right before Christmas. This man came in the back of the church and sat down, way on the back row in the dark. We were singing carols. But then somebody noticed him and he was bent way over. He kept blowing his nose. Somebody said, 'He's crying.' Mr. Jameson said maybe he ought to go and ask him to leave because he was probably drunk, but then he said, 'Maybe he just feels that way.' I guess he was drunk, though, don't you?"

Through years to come, Kemp would wonder if Jessie didn't know all the time that was her dad sitting in the back, hearing about the "everlasting light," welling up with tears, for her, for

Christmas, for Sheila, for everything beautiful. Someday I'll ask her, he thought. Someday when she's forty or more, with a wonderful job or a wonderful husband and wonderful children, I'll say, Didn't you know it was me? And she won't have to be told what I mean; she'll just say, Yes, sure I did.

Marriage

Melanie Sumner

"Every night," she told the marriage counselor, "he drinks a glass of milk. When he's finished, he sets the empty glass on the kitchen counter and goes to bed. He does not rinse it out. I have asked him and asked him. I've asked nicely, and I've screamed. Why should I rinse his glass out for him every night? If I don't do it, it's the first thing I see in the morning, this disgusting milk scum. I've even asked him, 'Will you just put the glass in the sink?' but he won't."

The counselor looked at the husband, a balding, middle-aged man who sat with his hands in his lap, a pleasant expression on his face.

"Did you hear what she was saying?" asked the counselor.

"Yes," said the man, nodding first at him, and then at his wife, to acknowledge everyone present.

A moment of silence passed. The counselor made a note on his pad, reminding himself to pick up a gallon of milk after work. Then he made eye contact with the wife.

"There is something you need to understand," he said. "He will never, never stop drinking that glass of milk before he goes to bed, and he will never rinse it out. There is absolutely nothing you can do."

The woman looked surprised. Sometimes, even after the divorce, she would think about the counselor's words, marveling at his wisdom.

Laura, Linda, Sweetie Pie

Daniel Wallace

She went crazy, briefly, in the fall, and tried to kill him. He wrote a story about it. In the story her name was Maureen, and instead of putting little pieces of gravel in the chocolate cake she was making for him, he had her put little pieces of gravel—and glass—in a strawberry tart. Nice touch, he thought, the glass. *Glinting in the bright kitchen light.*

She recovered just as the story was appearing in a magazine, and she read it and sued him. He wrote about that too, finishing a short piece before the trial itself was over. In that story he wasn't an author and she wasn't formerly crazy, but everything else was just about the same. In the writing he was somehow able to eke out a happy ending, with her actually dropping the suit and coming back to him. He had his lawyers send her a copy, and when she read it, against the advice of her own counsel, she was moved. She dropped the suit and went back.

Her real name was Laura. In his stories, other than Maureen, it was Linda, Carol, Beth, Deirdre, and Sweetie Pie. In one story she went nameless, and in the novel her name was Emma Fairchild. But whatever the name, it was always unmistakably her. She was the star of just about everything he wrote, and when she wasn't the star, she made a cameo appearance; he gave her tiny walk-on parts, as though he were one of those nepotistic movie directors, the kind who employs his mistress and members of his family in every film he makes. But he wasn't a director; he was only a writer. Still, you knew who "the golden-haired girl" was when the narrator spotted her, even briefly, in the supermarket, or when, out of the corner of his eye, he spied a girl "with hair the color of sunshine."

For a period of time—almost overnight—he became famous, but then just as quickly he drifted off into a puzzling obscurity.

His mother often wondered why he never wrote about her, and one day she came out and asked him. He told her he was sorry and promptly wrote a story with his mother in it, although everybody could tell it wasn't his mother at all but Laura dressed up to look like his mother. It was the best he could do.

As for the woman Laura, she loved him, she just thought he wrote too much. So he wrote about that. In this story he changed things around so that he was a salesman who was passionately devoted to his craft, but everything else was just about true to the facts, and it won a prize.

Then one day she got sick and stayed that way for a long time. It was hard, but he wrote about it, indirectly: Laura was absent from his stories now, but all his other characters became ill with something. They coughed a lot and took long naps. As she got sicker and sicker, so did everybody else in his other world, until finally nobody in any of his stories ever got out of bed. They were a bedridden lot, and his stories were very dull.

Finally, of course, she died.

After the funeral, he sat down at his desk, picked up a pencil, and wrote, *And then one day she died.*

He looked at what he had written, and he didn't like it. At all.

She died one day, he wrote.

But he didn't like that either.

So he erased it all and, in a flurry of inspiration, wrote, *She got real sick but all of a sudden started feeling better.*

That was pretty good.

He had never seen her look so radiant.

Oh, yes!

And he lived, and she lived, and everybody lived happily ever after.

But that was a story.

The end.

Mexican car wreck

Luke Whisnant

A Ditch

Here is where: the slick wet curve off-camber, the blacktop pitted with patches and ruts, the yellow double line faded almost invisible. A ditch along either side; standing water stinking of rot and hot rubber and hogshit; dockweed, mullein, wild onion, a spray of tiny yellow flowers with faces turned up to the rain. Blue styrofoam Filet-o-Fish. Rusted barbed wire. Skidmarks like screaming. A body facedown in the ditch. Turn him over.

Bodies

Six bodies. One in the ditch. Two in the tobacco past the ditch. One on the blacktop, one across the curve with his head crushed against a fence post, one so far flung that he isn't found for a quarter hour, and then only because a small brown dog circles him, whimpering. Six bodies. Every single one of them thrown from the vehicle. It's a cultural thing, the sheriff says for TV; they won't wear their seatbelts. Seatbelts are not macho. And of course there's never no kind of excuse for riding in the back like that.

State troopers with a yellow measuring tape, marking points of impact. The *wump-skreet, wump-skreet* of windshield wipers on an idle ambulance. An EMT strapping up a sheet-wrapped stretcher, weeping.

A Witness

Name's Herbert Joslyn. I live up here about a quarter mile. I was the first on the scene. Just awful. I was in Korea and saw nothing worst. A head-on Mexican car wreck. These fellas lived right up the road and was good neighbors, even if they couldn't speak much English. It's their families I feel sorry for.

The state has turned its back on this road. This curve was never engineered right from Day 1, nor maintained either. Five times now I've complained, and twice they've had their engineers out here, but you see what all good that done. Hell, yes, you can quote me, but no photographs. I got a microchip in me that breaks cameras. You think I'm foolin' but I'm not.

Clothing

Goodwill blue jeans a size too big or too small. Used T-shirts, discolored under the arms, or frayed double knits in lurid colors. Greasy adjust-a-band baseball caps: grinning Indians, leaping Marlins. Holes in old gray socks. But the shoes are new, new Nikes, all six pairs, black or blue uppers with neon green trim, see-through soles with magic air pockets. So you can fly.

Not Mexico

It's just such a damn stereotype, you know? one of the cops says: Mexicans crammed into the back of a pickup truck. You just cringe when you see it. It's like white people wearing Bermuda shorts and pennyloafers or black people eating watermelon.

Watermelon, cucumbers, strawberries. Tobacco here, peaches in South Carolina. Tomatoes in Georgia. Back here late summer for the tobacco harvest. In-between times, roofing or landscaping. Living in a thirty-year-old mobile home up on cinder blocks, three to a room. Sending what they can back home to Guatemala or Honduras. Not Mexico.

The Other Driver

None of the dead has ID. That's one rumor. All of the dead have ID, but names won't be released until next of kin are notified. That's another rumor. The cops run a license check on the red truck and find the plate was stolen. They check the VIN. Nobody seems to know anything. The TV camera guys are sweating under clear plastic ponchos. The reporters touch up their lipstick, then do their stand-ups. Someone says on camera that this is the worst wreck in county history. Someone else says that's bull. The cops tell the media people to take a hike, to clear out and let them do their jobs. The media people say they have a job to do too, give them a break, they're on deadline. One or another of them shake their heads, disgusted. Cops vs. reporters: it's a little dance they could do in their sleep.

The other driver sits in the rain on the running board of his dump truck, head in hands. The raindrops on his face make it hard to tell if he's crying. They slid into my lane, he says over and over. I stood on the brakes but couldn't get it stopped. I wasn't going any faster than 50, I swear to God. The TV people, shooed away by sheriff's deputies, scatter and stand aside a moment, then nonchalantly regroup around the dump truck, shooting surreptitiously from the hip.

Thrown Clear

In their pockets: a CP&L electric bill for $58.73 stamped "Paid." Cheap Food Lion sunglasses. Camels in crush-proof packs, crushed. Twenty-dollar bills, five-dollar bills, wads of ones, loose change, two Mexican pesos, a Honduran fifty centavo. A plastic toothpick dispenser. A roll of breath mints. A silver and turquoise ring. A three-pack of condoms, ribbed, and another three-pack, lubricated. A pocket watch with the crystal smashed.

Thrown clear: an English-Spanish phrase book. A requinto, a four-string guitar shaped from an armadillo shell. Five loads of dirty laundry in black milk crates. A black tarp the size of a pickup bed. The limping brown dog scuffling and whimpering around the ambulances.

Reverse

The moment of death hovers over the dead: weightless, a song no one hears, the moment of death and the moment before. It doesn't matter who believes this. It's true. Here, at the edge of a field a thousand miles from home, their moment is hovering. If you could put the truck in reverse, if driving backward were like rewinding a tape, you could enter the moment before: the moment of bliss, absolute and immutable. You could know what it meant to huddle with your compadres under a flapping tarp, tasting the summer drizzle on your face, glad that the rain had given you a day off so you could ride into town and do laundry. You could sing with your best friend the happy words about the banker's dark-haired daughter and the poor country boy, harmonizing over the high thrum of the requinto. You could roar with laughter, help-less, hugging the neck of the man next to you, gasping and weep-ing tears of joy at the dog—the dog singing along in his mournful howls and yelps, this pathetic wonderful North American singing dog.

And then the moment gone in an instant, the panicked creature sliding and scrambling, skittering with his long toenails across the metal bed of the truck, and everyone shouting as you head into the curve.

Alphabet soufflé

Lynn York

Anyway you cut it, Quentin, the youthful master chef and kingpin of Restaurante Que, was in big trouble. **B**ecause the green grocer had refused to make delivery for the week, Quentin was forced to operate on the dwindling pantry options: canned red peppers and artichokes, dried herbs, some fabulous olive oil, and a little pasta. **C**onservatively speaking, the meat in the locker would last until Tuesday, but after that, there would be nothing more until the butcher restored his credit.

During lunch service, several of the wait staff remarked on the condition of the lettuce. **E**ven the dishwashers looked askance, whispering among themselves while Quentin attempted to salt a watery potage. **F**ear, Quentin swore to himself, would not become part of his menu. **G**astronomy was his life's calling. **H**owever dire his circumstances, he would maintain a positive, upscale attitude, though he had to admit, his pastry chef Zoey had now made this nearly impossible.

Insisting on the best ingredients for each of her desserts was Zoey's trademark. **J**ust last month, she had actually requested gold foil—real gold leaf—to decorate her chocolate sin cake. **K**ingpin Quentin, though unaccustomed to such extravagance, liked to think of himself as a benevolent dictator, and he could not resist Zoey, who made the request with a flourish of her apron, powdered sugar clinging strategically to the front of her shirt. **L**iquidity and common sense departed, and she got her gold leaf.

Maybe that was where the trouble started. **N**o one else on staff asked for gold leaf, but the next week, the fresh truffles caught Quentin's eye. **O**ysters followed—the farm-raised variety from the

Gulf Coast. Pretty soon, Quentin could not restrain himself with the wine merchant, the caviar vendor, in the rare cheese section. Quentin extended his credit with every supplier in town. Resisting further extravagances became impossible. Several local food critics noted the change, however, and soon reservations were pouring in. Tables became scarce. Unusual and trendy personages began to reserve at Restaurante Que. Very soon, it occurred to Quentin that perhaps his prices did not match his escalating costs. Why this did not occur to him from the outset was not clear, though the lapse could be attributed to his growing infatuation with Zoey and her clingy high-quality hyperspun sugar.

Xerxes couldn't save him now.

Youth and fiscal overconfidence were Quentin's downfall.

Zoey left on the day he opened the last of the canned red peppers.

Contributors

MAX STEELE (1922–2005) directed the University of North Carolina at Chapel Hill's Creative Writing Program for twenty years before he retired in 1988. His work includes the novel *The Goblins Must Go Barefoot*, which won the Harper Prize; two short story collections, *Where She Brushed Her Hair* and *The Hat of My Mother*; and the children's book *The Cat and the Coffee Drinkers*. The recipient of two O. Henry Awards, he was also an editor at *Story Magazine* and the *Paris Review* and mentored countless young writers who launched successful literary careers themselves.

ANTHONY S. ABBOTT, professor emeritus of English at Davidson College, is the author of two novels, *Leaving Maggie Hope* and *The Three Great Secret Things*. He has also written four books of poems, the most recent of which, *The Man Who*, won the Oscar Arnold Young Award from the North Carolina Poetry Council.

DAPHNE ATHAS has written fiction, essays, poetry, and travel narratives. *Entering Ephesus* appeared on *Time* magazine's Ten Best Fiction list. *Gram-O-Rama*, her most recent project, is an online and print text for colleges and high schools on grammar as performance art. She teaches writing at the University of North Carolina at Chapel Hill.

RUSSELL BANKS, the first member of his family to attend college, graduated Phi Beta Kappa from the University of North Carolina at Chapel Hill. A prolific writer of fiction, his award-winning titles include *The Sweet Hereafter*, *Affliction*, *Cloudsplitter*, *Rule of the Bone*, and *The Angel on the Roof*. His most recent books are *The Reserve* and *Dreaming Up America*. He has been the recipient of numerous literary prizes and accolades, including the John Dos Passos Award and the Literature Award from the American Academy of Arts and Letters.

WILTON BARNHARDT is a former reporter for *Sports Illustrated* and the author of *Emma Who Saved My Life*, *Gospel*, and *Show World*. He teaches fiction writing to undergraduate and graduate students at North Carolina

State University, where he is the director of the MFA program in creative writing.

DORIS BETTS was for thirty-three years a member of the English/creative writing faculty at the University of North Carolina at Chapel Hill, retiring in 2001 as alumni distinguished professor. She has published nine books of fiction, most recently *The Sharp Teeth of Love.*

WILL BLYTHE, a former literary editor at *Esquire* magazine, writes for many other periodicals, including *Harper's, The New Yorker, Sports Illustrated,* and *Rolling Stone.* A graduate of the University of North Carolina at Chapel Hill, he is perhaps best known for his book, *To Hate Like This Is to Be Happy Forever,* which explores the intense rivalry between Duke and Carolina basketball fans.

WENDY BRENNER is the author of two short story collections and a recipient of the Flannery O'Connor Award. Her work has appeared in *Seventeen, Allure,* and other magazines and in *Best America Magazine Writing 2006.* She teaches in the MFA program at the University of North Carolina at Wilmington.

AMY KNOX BROWN is a fourth-generation Nebraskan currently living in Winston-Salem, North Carolina, where she is an assistant professor of English and creative writing at Salem College and the director of the college's creative writing major. She is the author of the short story collection *Three Versions of the Truth* and the poetry chapbook *Advice from Household Gods.*

BEKAH BRUNSTETTER hails from Winston-Salem, North Carolina. She received her BA in theater with honors in fiction writing from the University of North Carolina at Chapel Hill, winning the Selden Prize for best original drama script, the Rubin Prize for Fiction, and the Willie Lavonsa Moore Prize for Nonfiction. She received an MFA in dramatic writing from the New School for Drama.

ORSON SCOTT CARD has lived in Greensboro, North Carolina, for twenty-five years, where he writes two columns for the *Rhinoceros Times.* He has written more than fifty books, including *Ender's Game, Lost Boys,* and *Sarah,* and publishes the online poetry magazine *StrongVerse.org.*

FRED CHAPPELL, a native of Canton in the mountains of western North Carolina, taught writing and literature at the University of North Carolina at Greensboro for thirty years until his retirement in 2005. He is the author of more than a dozen books of verse, two short story collections, and eight novels. Former poet laureate of North Carolina, he is the winner of, among other awards, the Bollingen Prize in Poetry, the Aiken Taylor Prize, the T. S. Eliot Prize, the Roanoke-Chowan Prize seven times over, and the Caroliniana Award for Lifetime Achievement in Literature.

KELLY CHERRY's most recent titles are *Girl in a Library*, *Hazard and Prospect: New and Selected Poems*, and the forthcoming poetry collection *The Retreats of Thought*. Her fiction has appeared in *Best American Short Stories*, *Prize Stories: The O. Henry Awards*, *The Pushcart Prize*, and *New Stories from the South*. She received an MFA from the University of North Carolina at Greensboro and now lives in Southside, Virginia.

ELIZABETH COX is the author of four novels, including *Night Talk*, which won the Lillian Smith Award for raising social consciousness and promoting harmony between the races, and *The Slow Moon*. She also published a book of short stories, *Bargains in the Real World*. Cox taught creative writing at Duke University for seventeen years. She now shares (with her husband Michael Curtis) the John Cobb Chair of Humanities at Wofford College in Spartanburg, South Carolina.

QUINN DALTON, who lives in Greensboro, North Carolina, is the author of a novel, *High Strung*, and two short story collections, *Bulletproof Girl* and *Stories from the Afterlife*. Her short stories and essays have appeared in literary magazines such as *One Story*, *Verb*, and *Glimmer Train* and in anthologies such as *New Stories from the South*. Her website is www.quinndalton .com.

ANGELA DAVIS-GARDNER is the author of the novels *Butterfly's Child*, *Plum Wine*, *Forms of Shelter*, and *Felice* and is at work on a collection of linked short-short stories. A distinguished professor emerita of creative writing at North Carolina State University, she lives in Raleigh with an award-winning family and several imaginary pets.

SARAH DESSEN grew up in Chapel Hill, North Carolina, and is the author of eight award-winning books for young adults, including *Just Listen* and *Lock and Key*, which have enjoyed immense popularity as *New York Times* best sellers. A new novel, *Along for the Ride*, is forthcoming. She lives in Chapel Hill.

PAMELA DUNCAN is the author of three novels, *Moon Women*, *Plant Life*, and *The Big Beautiful*. She holds a BA in journalism from the University of North Carolina at Chapel Hill and an MA in English/creative writing from North Carolina State University. She teaches creative writing at Western Carolina University.

PAM DURBAN is the author of two novels and a collection of short stories. Her story "Soon" was included in *The Best American Short Stories of the Century*. She is the first Doris Betts Distinguished Professor of Creative Writing at the University of North Carolina at Chapel Hill.

CLYDE EDGERTON is the author of several novels, including *Raney*, *Walking Across Egypt*, *Lunch at the Piccadilly*, and *The Bible Salesman*. He teaches in the Creative Writing Department at the University of North Carolina at Wilmington.

TRACIE FELLERS is a native of Durham, North Carolina, and a freelance writer and editor who started her career writing for daily newspapers in North Carolina and Virginia. She is a graduate of Northwestern University, North Carolina State University, and the University of North Carolina at Greensboro. Her fiction has appeared in *Roger*, and she has published creative nonfiction in the journal *Sing Heavenly Muse!* She has received awards for her fiction from NCSU and the National Council for Black Studies.

BEN FOUNTAIN was born in Chapel Hill but grew up in eastern North Carolina and currently lives in Texas. His short story collection *Encounters with Ché Guevara* received the PEN/Hemingway Award. He is also the recipient of a Whiting Writer's Award, an O'Henry Award, and two Pushcart Prizes, among other honors.

PHILIP GERARD is the author of three novels and four books of nonfiction, as well as numerous documentary scripts, short stories, essays, and the historical radio drama, *1898: An American Coup*. He is professor and chair of creative writing at the University of North Carolina at Wilmington, where he has made his home since 1989.

MARIANNE GINGHER has published seven books, both fiction and nonfiction, most recently *Adventures in Pen Land*, a comic memoir about the experiences that led her to write her first novel, *Bobby Rex's Greatest Hit*. She proudly edited the anthology that you are browsing. A former director of the

Creative Writing Program there, she has taught at the University of North Carolina at Chapel Hill for more than twenty-five years.

GAIL GODWIN grew up in Asheville, North Carolina, and was educated at Peace College and the University of North Carolina at Chapel Hill. A three-time finalist for the National Book Award, she has published thirteen novels, two short story collections, a young writer's diary, and a nonfiction work on the heart. Her archives are in the Southern Historical Collection at the University of North Carolina at Chapel Hill.

JIM GRIMSLEY is a North Carolina native and graduate of the University of North Carolina at Chapel Hill and the author of nine novels, a book of plays, and a collection of short stories. He lives and writes in Decatur, Georgia, and teaches writing at Emory University.

VIRGINIA HOLMAN, the author of the memoir *Rescuing Patty Hearst*, lives and kayaks in Carolina Beach, North Carolina.

RANDALL KENAN is the author of two works of fiction, *A Visitation of Spirits* and *Let the Dead Bury Their Dead*, and three works of nonfiction, including *Walking on Water: Black American Lives at the Turn of the Twenty-first Century* and *The Fire This Time*. He is an associate professor of English at the University of North Carolina at Chapel Hill.

JOHN KESSEL codirects the Creative Writing Program at North Carolina State University. A winner of the Nebula, Theodore Sturgeon, and Tiptree Awards, his books include *Good News from Outer Space*, *Corrupting Dr. Nice*, *The Pure Product*, and, most recently, *The Baum Plan for Financial Independence and Other Stories*.

HAVEN KIMMEL was raised in Indiana, the focus of her best-selling memoir, *A Girl Named Zippy: Growing up Small in Mooreland, Indiana*. She earned her graduate degree in creative writing from North Carolina State University, where she studied with novelist Lee Smith. She is the author of *The Solace of Leaving Early*, *Something Rising (Light and Swift)*, and *The Used World*, her "trilogy of place" about fictional Hopwood County, Indiana. Her other works include a second memoir, *She Got Up Off the Couch*; a poetic children's book, *Orville: A Dog Story*; and the novel *Iodine*.

CARRIE KNOWLES grew up near Detroit but was raised a southerner, her father being from Georgia and her mother from the Ozarks. She has lived with her husband, Jeff Leiter, in Raleigh, North Carolina, for thirty years. Her fiction has appeared in *The Sun*, the *Raleigh News and Observer*, and *Glimmer Train*.

TELISHA MOORE LEIGG, the mother of toddler-age twin boys, teaches magazine journalism and Japanese in Danville, Virginia. She has owned a home in Ruffin, North Carolina, since 1996 and received her MFA in creative writing from Warren Wilson College, where she came under the "kind influence of Wilton Barnhardt." She has published short stories in *The William and Mary Gallery of Writing, Jump!*, and *Primavera*.

PETER MAKUCK is a distinguished professor emeritus at East Carolina University and the founder and editor of *Tar River Poetry* from 1978 to 2006. He has had short stories, poems, essays, and reviews in the *Hudson Review*, the *Sewanee Review*, and *Poetry*. His most recent collection of short stories is *Costly Habits*.

MICHAEL MALONE's short stories are collected in *Red Clay, Blue Cadillac*. His novels include *Handling Sin, Uncivil Seasons, Time's Witness, The Last Noel*, and the forthcoming *The Four Corners of the Sky*. Winner of the O'Henry, Edgar, Emmy, and Writer's Guild Awards, he teaches theater studies at Duke University.

DOUG MARLETTE (1949–2007) was born in Greensboro, North Carolina, and wrote and drew the nationally syndicated comic strip *Kudzu*, which he created in 1981. During his lifetime, he won every major award for editorial cartooning, including the 1988 Pulitzer Prize. The author of two novels, *The Bridge* and *Magic Time*, he was awarded, posthumously, membership in the Order of the Long Leaf Pine, the highest civilian honor bestowed by the governor of North Carolina.

MARGARET MARON is a native Tar Heel who still lives on a corner of the family farm and is the author of twenty-four novels and dozens of short stories. She has served as president of Sisters in Crime, Mystery Writers of America, and the American Crime Writers League.

JILL MCCORKLE is the author of five novels, including *The Cheer Leader* and *Carolina Moon*, and three short story collections, most recently *Creatures of Habit*. Her work has appeared in the *Atlantic*, *Ploughshares*, *Best American Short Stories*, and *New Stories from the South*. The recipient of the

New England Book Award, the John Dos Passos Prize, and the North Carolina Award for Literature, she has taught creative writing at the University of North Carolina at Chapel Hill, Tufts University, Harvard University, Brandeis University, and Bennington College. She is currently on the faculty at North Carolina State University.

PHILIP MCFEE was born in Durham, North Carolina. A graduate of the University of North Carolina at Chapel Hill and a winner of the Max Steele Award for Fiction Writing, he was nominated for a Pushcart Prize for work that appeared in *Inch*. He currently lives in Cleveland, Ohio, where he freelances as a design consultant.

JOHN MCNALLY is the author of five works of fiction, *The Last Semester*, *Ghosts of Chicago*, *America's Report Card*, *The Book of Ralph*, and *Troublemakers*. He and his wife, Amy Knox Brown, live in Winston-Salem, North Carolina, where John is associate professor of English at Wake Forest University.

HEATHER ROSS MILLER, with over a dozen published books, writes fiction, poetry, and nonfiction. Retired from Washington and Lee University as the first Thomas Broadus Distinguished Professor, she currently teaches part-time at Pfeiffer University in Charlotte, North Carolina.

LYDIA MILLET, a graduate of the University of North Carolina at Chapel Hill, is the author of six novels, most recently *How the Dead Dream*. Her fifth novel, *Oh Pure and Radiant Heart*, was short-listed for Britain's Arthur C. Clarke Prize; her fourth, *My Happy Life*, won the PEN-USA Award. Millet lives in the desert outside of Tucson, Arizona.

KATHERINE MIN's works include the novel *Secondhand World*. Her short stories have appeared in many magazines, including *Tri-Quarterly*, *Ploughshares*, and *Prairie Schooner*. She has won a Pushcart Prize and received grants from the National Endowment for the Arts and the New Hampshire State Council in the Arts. She currently teaches at the University of North Carolina at Asheville.

COURTNEY JONES MITCHELL's fiction has appeared in *Best New American Voices (2004)*, *Carolina Quarterly*, the *Raleigh News and Observer*, and the *Carrboro Free Press*. She lives with her husband in Chapel Hill and is working on a novel.

RUTH MOOSE is a poet and fiction writer who teaches writing at the University of North Carolina at Chapel Hill. Her two collections of short stories are *The Wreath Ribbon Quilt* and *Dreaming in Color*. Her latest volumes of poetry are *Making the Bed* and *The Sleepwalker*.

ROBERT MORGAN is a native of Henderson County, North Carolina, and has published three books of poetry and five novels, including *Gap Creek* and *Brave Enemies: A Novel of the American Revolution*. He is also the author of a nonfiction work, *Boone: A Biography*. Since 1971 he has taught at Cornell University, where he is currently Kappa Alpha Professor of English.

SHELIA MOSES was raised the ninth of ten children on Rehobeth Road in Rich Square, North Carolina. She is coauthor of Dick Gregory's memoir, *Callus on My Soul*, as well as the author of six books for young adults, including *I, Dred Scott: A Fictional Slave Narrative Based on the Life and Legal Precedent of Dred Scott*, *The Legend of Buddy Bush*, *The Return of Buddy Bush*, and *The Baptism: Sallie Gal and the Wall-kee-Man and Joseph*. A National Book Award finalist and Coretta Scott King Honors Award winner, Moses is currently writing a young adult book about Barack Obama. She lives in Atlanta, Georgia.

LAWRENCE NAUMOFF, a Charlotte native and graduate of the University of North Carolina at Chapel Hill, is the author of six novels, including *Rootie Kazootie*, *Silk Hope*, and *Taller Women*. He teaches creative writing at the University of North Carolina at Chapel Hill. His website is www.lawrencenaumoff.com.

JENNY OFFILL is the author of the novel *Last Things*, as well as the coeditor, along with Elissa Schappell, of two anthologies, *The Friend Who Got Away* and *Money Changes Everything*. Her first children's book is *17 Things I'm Not Allowed To Do Anymore*. She currently teaches fiction writing at Brooklyn College, Columbia University, and the low-residency MFA program at Queens University in Charlotte, North Carolina.

ELIZABETH OLIVER's fiction has appeared in publications including *Sundog*, the *Southeast Review*, *Puerto del Sol*, and *SmokeLong Quarterly*. Founder, along with her husband, of *The Rambler* magazine, she lives in Apex and works in Pittsboro, North Carolina.

MICHAEL PARKER was born in Siler City, North Carolina; grew up in Clinton; and, since 1992, has taught in the MFA writing program at the University of North Carolina at Greensboro. He has published six works of fiction, most recently the novel *If You Want Me to Stay* and the short story collection *Don't Make Me Stop Now.*

PEGGY PAYNE is the author of the novels *Sister India* and *Revelation*, among other books. She has published in the *New York Times*, the *Washington Post*, *Cosmopolitan*, *More*, *Family Circle*, *Travel & Leisure*, and elsewhere. She lives in Raleigh, North Carolina, and is also a consultant to other writers, offering manuscript feedback and career strategies. Her website is www.peggypayne.com.

JOE ASHBY PORTER, author of seven books of fiction, has taught writing since 1980 at Duke University.

DENISE RICKMAN won a National Gold Key Award for her story "Egg Girl," which was included in *The Best Teen Writing of 2006*. She received the University of North Carolina at Chapel Hill's Thomas Wolfe Scholarship and is currently an undergraduate in residence at Chapel Hill. She won the 2008 Mini-Max prize for her short-short "The Onion Girl."

DAVID ROWELL was born and raised in Fayetteville, North Carolina, and graduated from the University of North Carolina at Chapel Hill. He is an editor at the *Washington Post Magazine* and lives in Silver Spring, Maryland, with his wife and two sons.

JOHN ROWELL, David's brother, also grew up in Fayetteville, North Carolina, and graduated from the University of North Carolina at Chapel Hill, where he studied creative writing with Max Steele and Daphne Athas. John also holds an MFA from the Writing Seminars at Bennington College. His short story collection, *The Music of Your Life*, was short-listed for the Publishing Triangle's Ferro-Gumley Award as best fiction book of the year. John's work has appeared in *Tin House* and *Bloom*, among other journals. He currently lives and teaches in Baltimore.

DEBORAH SEABROOKE is originally from Long Island but has lived in Greensboro, North Carolina, for thirty-five years. She graduated from the University of North Carolina at Greensboro's MFA program, where she studied with Fred Chappell. Her fiction has appeared in the *Virginia Re-*

view, the *Greensboro Review*, *Best American Short Stories*, and, most recently, the chapbook *Margins of Error*. About every other year, she and her husband take off to Italy, working on farms for room and board.

DAVE SHAW's first book won the Katherine Anne Porter Prize, and his second was runner-up for the Richard Sullivan Award. He holds an MFA from the University of North Carolina at Greensboro and teaches at the University of North Carolina at Chapel Hill, where he is executive editor of *Southern Cultures*.

BLAND SIMPSON, Bowman and Gordon Gray Professor of English and Creative Writing at the University of North Carolina at Chapel Hill, is a longtime member of the Tony Award–winning Red Clay Ramblers. Collaborator on such musicals as *Diamond Studs*, *King Mackerel*, and *Kudzu* and author of *Into the Sound Country* and *The Inner Islands*, with photography by his wife, Ann Cary Simpson, he has received the North Carolina Award in Fine Arts.

LEE SMITH is the author of eleven novels, including *Oral Histories, Saving Grace, The Devil's Dream, Fair and Tender Ladies,* and *On Agate Hill,* plus three collections of short stories. Her novel *The Last Girls* was a *New York Times* best seller as well as a winner of the Southern Book Critics Circle Award. A retired professor of English at North Carolina State University, Smith received an Academy Award in Fiction from the American Academy of Arts and Letters.

JUNE SPENCE is the author of the novel *Change Baby* and the short story collection *Missing Women and Others*. She is from Raleigh, North Carolina, where she lives with her husband, writer Scott Huler, and their two sons.

ELIZABETH SPENCER has published seventeen books of fiction, including *The Salt Line, Night Travelers, Jack of Diamonds and Other Stories, The Southern Woman,* and *The Light in The Piazza,* on which the hit Broadway musical was based. She is a five-time recipient of the O. Henry Award for Short Fiction. Other awards include the John Dos Passos Award for Literature, the North Carolina Governor's Award for Literature, and the Thomas Wolfe Award for Literature, given by the University of North Carolina at Chapel Hill. She is a member of the American Institute of Arts and Letters.

MELANIE SUMNER graduated from the University of North Carolina at Chapel Hill with a BA in religious studies and returned to teach creative writing from 1995 to 1996. She is the author of *The School of Beauty and Charm* and *Polite Society* and the recipient of a Whiting Award. Her short stories and essays have been published in many venues, including *The New Yorker*, the *New York Times*, *Harper's*, *Ladies Home Journal*, and *Seventeen*, as well as being widely anthologized. She is currently teaching creative writing at Kennesaw State University.

DANIEL WALLACE has published four novels, most recently *Mr. Sebastian and the Negro Magician*. He graduated from the University of North Carolina at Chapel Hill and now teaches in the Creative Writing Department there.

LUKE WHISNANT is the author of *Watching TV with the Red Chinese*, a novel, and *Down in the Flood*, a collection of short stories. He grew up in Charlotte and has taught creative writing at East Carolina University since 1982.

LYNN YORK is a native North Carolinian and the author of two novels, *The Piano Teacher* and *The Sweet Life*. She lives in Carrboro, North Carolina.

Permissions

"The Playhouse," by Max Steele, previously appeared in *Black Warrior Review* 24, no. 2 (1998) and *Harper's Magazine* (December 1998). Copyright 1998 by Max Steele. Reprinted by permission of Oliver Steele, Literary Executor of the Estate of Henry Maxwell Steele.

"The Roommate," by Anthony S. Abbott. Copyright 2009 by Anthony S. Abbott.

"Games," by Daphne Athas. Copyright 2009 by Daphne Athas.

"The Outer Banks," by Russell Banks, previously appeared in *Angel on the Roof* (HarperCollins, 2000). Copyright 2000 by Russell Banks. Reprinted by permission of the author and HarperCollins Publishers.

"Stoma," by Wilton Barnhardt. Copyright 2009 by Wilton Barnhardt.

"The Girl Who Wanted to Be a Horse," by Doris Betts. Copyright 2009 by Doris Betts.

"The End," by Will Blythe. Copyright 2009 by Will Blythe.

"Nipple," by Wendy Brenner, previously appeared in *Five Points* (Spring/ Summer 1997) and *New Stories from the South* (Algonquin Books, 1998). Copyright 1998 by Wendy Brenner. Reprinted by permission of the author and Algonquin Books.

"Aeneus Leaves Kansas," by Amy Knox Brown, previously appeared in *Three Versions of the Truth* (Press 53, 2007). Copyright 2007 by Amy Knox Brown. Reprinted by permission of the author and Press 53.

"hey brother," by Bekah Brunstetter. Copyright 2009 by Bekah Brunstetter.

"Very Bad Children," by Orson Scott Card. Copyright 2009 by Orson Scott Card.

"January," by Fred Chappell, previously appeared in *Moments of Light* (New South Company, 1980). Copyright 1980 by Fred Chappell. Reprinted by permission of the author.

"Where Love Is," by Kelly Cherry, previously appeared as a section in "Chapters of a Dog's Life," *Society of Friends: Stories* (University of Missouri Press, 1999). Copyright 1999 by Kelly Cherry. Reprinted by permission of the author.